FIRES

FIRES

a novel

Nick Antosca

IM·PE·TUS
press

Impetus Press
PO Box 10025
Iowa City, IA 52240
www.impetuspress.com
info@impetuspress.com

Copyright © 2006 Nick Antosca. All rights reserved.

This book is a work of fiction. Names, characters, businesses, organizations, places, events, and incidents either are the product of the author's imagination or are used fictitiously. Any resemblance to actual persons, living or dead, events, or locales is entirely coincidental.

ISBN 0-9776693-2-7

cover design and text layout
by Willy Blackmore

cover photo
by Jennifer Banash

December 2006
Printed in Canada

for Booth

> I knew what it was, but I pretended not to; I refused to look at it, and put it out of my memory.
>
> —*The Confessions of St. Augustine*

> In the end, he had to rescue himself from Mann Gulch by asking to be transferred to another ranger district. It had got so that he could not sleep at night, remembering the smell of it, and his dog would no longer come in but cried all night outside, knowing that something had gone wrong with him.
>
> —*Young Men and Fire*
> Norman Maclean

The radio says mountains are on fire. I wake beside Ruth, kicking off sweat-damp sheets, careful not to jostle her. She's still passed out, thank God. It's ten AM. The heat is homicidal.

I fumble for the radio and turn it off.

Mountains—the green, densely forested mountains behind my old neighborhood—are burning. The Appalachians. No rain all spring. Dry lightning storms have whispered across Maryland and Virginia, igniting undergrowth, birthing infant forest fires that have become monstrous in adulthood. Fires like these are unheard-of on the East Coast; they've been headlines for days.

The development where I grew up has been evacuated. My parents are waiting it out in Atlantic City.

But I don't want to think about my parents. Or the fire.

I sit up carefully beside Ruth.

Dorm beds are designed for a single person, so if you're sharing one with a girl you're in love, or lust, with, the bed is perfect, because you have to be practically on top of her. But if you're not supposed to be there at all—if the other person doesn't know you're there—things aren't as simple.

I'm thinking about Ruth and her brother.

I'm thinking about James Dearborn. And George Mursey. And a room behind a basement wall.

The sun is glowing, the window open. I hear voices on the green. Kids playing frisbee and lounging on the grass, half-dressed. Flirting. Laughing.

Ruth will wake up soon. I need to get out of here before she does.

She is lying passed out with her face smashed into the pillow, shoulders bare and insolent, tangled dark hair bunched up at her neck. Her breathing is irregular. She's beautiful, in a messy, bare-shouldered, morning breath way. Mocha-colored moles form constellations on her shoulder blades. The sunlight clings to her knotted hair.

James Dearborn is someone I know from high school.

And George Mursey is a big, affable guy from my home town, a neighbor from just across the street. A high school teacher, a football coach. Not a guy you'd expect to—

Wait. I don't want to think about it yet.

I want to think about Ruth.

Ruth

Go back a few months.

Winter's almost over but the air has teeth. Coldest season in years; even in gloves my fingers are numb. The bells of Harkness Tower ring boredly, endlessly. I'm wandering the New Haven streets wanting to do something, kick something, burn something—but I push those things down, because I am very good at pushing things down. I hate the winter here. I'm nostalgic for home, autumn: neighborhood streets, the smell of burning leaves, the taste of grass in the air. Dusk becomes night. I see a dead cat. I was going to have dinner with someone, but she didn't show.

So now I have that feeling of being a loose pinball—helpless, displaced, obscurely afraid. And I keep wandering cold dark streets, looking for someone I know. Anyone. I need that. I don't like to be alone.

Finally I sit on a cracked bench outside William Harkness Hall. Beside me, like a friend, sits a naked baby doll. I lose a short but intense staring contest with it. Unnerved, I take refuge inside the building. In an empty seminar room, I peel off my gloves. The knuckles are cracked and white-fringed like old carrots.

I step back into the hallway. Voices drift. People studying, debating, rehearsing. I feel like I'm not really a student here. Like I'm someone who ought to have been kicked out, but coffee got spilled on the paperwork. From nearby a sweet voice rises, joined by others, and I creep up to the doorway it's coming from. Religious a cappella. I back away, confused.

Blowing on my hands, I go upstairs. Music comes from a classroom: the soundtrack from an old musical, with lyrics about murder. I drift to the door, look in.

A film's being screened on a video projector. The musical bit ends and Woody Allen and a young woman walk down a city street. A movie within a movie. I slip into the room. The audience, students slumped in desk chairs, ignores me. This will do.

It's dark in the room—my knees thud on things—but I find a seat. Beside me, a lumpish bundle of winter clothes sniffles, harrumphs. Clears its throat.

I watch the movie. I'm barely paying attention, but it seems to involve Mussolini and Mister Ed. Infantile snuffling noises come out of the lump beside me, and I deduce that the lump is female and probably contagious. Further details are hidden by a shapeless jacket and knit cap.

Afterward, a professor with scary liver spots shuffles up front to talk, but the students herd for the door. The female lump doesn't move except to rub its nose. I rise and slip out the door. The hall empties. Departing footsteps echo.

I go into the men's room and light a cigarette, feeling somehow defeated and mocked. Defeat is one thing, mockery is another. I stare at the tiles.

Finishing my cigarette, I crush it in the sink and light another. When I step back into the hall, sighing smoke, the classroom where they just screened the movie is empty. I peer inside. Someone has forgotten a pair of gloves. The building feels tomb-like. Thursday night, everyone's out drinking.

Water gurgles. The congested, red-nosed lump of a girl emerges from the women's room, shoulders bowed under a heavy backpack. She's trumpeting into a paper towel that's crumpled to her face.

Can I have one? she says. She lowers the paper towel. Pursed, damp lips.

I offer the pack. Even as she takes a cigarette, she's coughing, breath rattling in her chest like eggshells.

You shouldn't smoke if you're sick.

Yeah, she says as she strikes a paper match. Uh-huh.

Burns up your throat.

Oh, my throat can take it. She looks up at me, eyes glistening, and shakes out the match. My throat has a history of violence, okay?

Fair enough.

We walk down the hall, not sure if we're walking together or just walking the same way. Dark hair has worked loose from her cap and is sticking to her cheeks. She seems familiar and maybe I've seen her before.

ANTOSCA

You're not in the class, she says.
I know.
But you were next to me at the screening.
Yeah.
You have a colorful social life, going to screenings on Thursday nights for classes you aren't taking.

I chew my lip as we go down the stairs, wondering if I'm being baited into flirtatious verbal sparring or just insulted, and whether I would even bother flirting with her on a different night, if I weren't so lonely. She tosses her cigarette against the wall. Sparks jump at our feet. Sniffling, she turns to me and lifts an eyebrow; there's something both obscene and contrived about it.

Can I have another?

She lights up again on the first floor. We go out the double doors and pause in the frigid night. I look around and at my feet as she smokes. The weight of her backpack makes her stand off-balance. We face a dark, empty quad. Beside us there's a bike rack and a bulletin board where tatters of colored paper cling. Some subtle curve in the shape of the girl's eyes—wide as almonds—appears alien, like tundra animal eyes transplanted into a human face.

I blow into my cupped hands, realizing I left my gloves inside. But I don't want to break this off, so I keep silent. She looks at the sky and blows commas of smoke into the darkness.

Who are you? she says.
My name's Jon.

Dim, raucous shouts rise in the distance. Cars rumble on a nearby street, branches scrape windows—the sound of silence in a city where nothing is ever silent. How different this is from home. Numbness creeps into my fingers.

Yours?
Ruth.

FIRES

She blows smoke at the moon, huddled up like a vagrant.

A streetlight shows the redness in her cheeks. Pink earlobes peek out below her cap, and her brown eyes glisten.

You've got what's going around. That bug.

It's a nasty one. This germ can do the pole vault. But once you've had it, I hear you don't get it again. You been sick yet?

I probably am now. Don't worry about it.

Neither of us says anything. A pathetic, rat-like squirrel hops across the grass, quivering weirdly. There's something wrong with the squirrels in New Haven. Ruth tosses her cigarette against the bike rack. Embers scatter.

My nose is numb, she complains. Dark brown eyes, turning to watch me. Your hands must be fucking freezing, she says. Don't you have gloves?

No, I say. So what are you doing now? Hibernating til Monday?

Going to a party.

Really. Where at?

An apartment.

Ah. Yes. An apartment.

She chews her lips, sniffles. If I liked you, she mutters as if thinking out loud, I might invite you along.

And if I cared enough to be insulted by that, I'd . . . I'd . . .

He's so quick with the comeback.

Fuck off.

She rocks on her heels—awkward with that heavy backpack—and leans toward me, in confidence.

Come on, she says, there's no reason you should be insulted.

When people insult me, I'm insulted. I can't help it. That's just me. That's just this condition I have.

I didn't insult you.

You said you dislike me, but fine, fair enough, I guess that's not technically an insult.

ANTOSCA

Oh, I just implied that—but you didn't wait to see if I would invite you.

She rocks on her heels again, looking pleased with herself. Girls who play games should be shipped off to an island with a volcano.

Out in the cold darkness, a fire engine. Glass shattering somewhere. A homeless guy shuffles across the grass, paying no attention.

I look back at Ruth, who is staring into the night. Her face is naked, cupped coldly by the streetlight. She seems to have forgotten where she is.

I murmur—Well?

I lapse into silence. A moment drags past.

Well? I repeat.

She turns to look at me.

The teasing, smart-aleck manner has vanished. Dark strands of hair garland her face. She grins a slow, crooked grin.

Sorry. I zoned. It's the medicine.

So? Party?

I'm sorry. I was just fucking with you.

Huh?

It's the cold medicine. And I haven't slept. I'm in a rotten mood.

So, uh, there's no party?

There is. Coming?

Were you fucking with me when you said you'd invite me if you liked me?

No. (She sniffles; her large brown eyes water.) You'll come? You'll come.

To Bed

An apartment I've been to before. Crown Street.

That hollow, helpless feeling I have on lonely nights begins to dissolve. It feels good to go into the party with Ruth.

This junior Zack and his roommates live here. The walls are covered with concert posters. A pennant that says "For God, For Country, and For Yale" is hung upside-down and looks like it's maybe been urinated on. Zack's dog, Jeffrey Dahmer, roots through the kitchen trash. He's the sweetest dog in the world.

The apartment smells like hickory-flavored tobacco. People are lying on the rug. Some guy traps me, starts talking about magnets and macrobiotics. Then he's talking about the media—a three-legged puppy, he says, walking in circles, eating its feces.

I catch up to Ruth by a chair piled with winter coats, where she's peeling off her jacket. Her body is svelte, slim hips and small breasts. Even in the relative light I won't hazard a guess about her ethnicity—she must be some sort of mongrel. The best-looking girls are strange mixes. I once met a half-Italian, half-Arab girl who had similar features, except that girl didn't have a light spray of freckles on her nose and cheekbones, like Ruth has.

Uncapping a bottle of Robitussin, she drinks, grins, and drifts away into the kitchen. I find myself smiling dumbly back, at nothing. I linger next to the sofa, feeling abandoned—but I don't want to start talking to anyone, because then Ruth might do the same and eventually forget about me. So I just hover awkwardly, clenching and unclenching my hands. After a moment, she floats back.

There's no more to drink, she says. They drank it all, the greedy swine.

With nowhere else to go, we sit on the rug. I feel foolish next to her, trying to arrange my legs, finally sitting Indian-style. Jeffrey Dahmer ambles up and affectionately nuzzles my crotch; I push him away. Around us, the sofas are draped with stoned people, like shelves of limp puppets.

Oh, and look at this. James Dearborn is here.

James. James, who lives just down the street from here above a Japanese place, sits across from us. He is smoking a Lucky Strike. His long lean body holds itself like a portrait, a certain wincing tension in the way his mouth has pursed. Someone is whispering in his ear. An actor, a popular gay actor, is whispering to him. But James is watching Ruth.

Ruth doesn't notice.

It is very convincing, the way she pretends not to notice.

We went to high school together, James and I. We grew up in the same neighborhood, even—I can actually remember being four or five years old and seeing him on the playground. Therefore we are required to nod at one another when we pass on the street. James was a year ahead of me until college, then took a year off; now we're both juniors. He is remembered at our high school, immortalized in a display case. Mythic feats of athleticism.

I once spent part of an afternoon hanging out with him, a long time ago now, and it made something of an impression on me. I wonder if he remembers.

Taking a rip off a large red bong with glass salamanders crawling up its sides, I lean against Ruth and let time slow down, relax.

My eyes pass over lovely shadows, gentle dark places; I'm relaxed and happily drugged. I'm touching her ankle with the backs of my fingers. I'm stoned, looking at girls as I murmur things to Ruth.

She doesn't laugh often—mostly sniffles and coughs, whimpering in self-pity—but when she does, her laugh is a raw, live thing that scrapes out of her chest and startles me. It occurs to me with a thrill that I might have stumbled, even if just for a night, onto someone sort of unique, someone who's not one of the New York prep school girls who infest the party scene like vermin, with their Burberry scarves and Gauloises. (I was shocked when I found out people actually smoke those; I thought it was only in novels, and even then only French homosexuals.)

Zack lounges on the sofa behind her—wearing, for some reason, a necklace of bird heads—and petting her hair. They must know each other, because she laughs and leans her soft dark head against his knee.

I feel a stab of jealousy.

Past fights with girlfriends flash back to me—jealousies, breathless violence in the air, a fear of what I might recklessly say or do—and I tell myself to calm down.

So I take a deep breath and watch Ruth (her head still pressed against Zack's leg, his fingers in her hair) because now she's watching me; we're making eye contact, and I notice that her pupils are the largest and most marble-black that I've ever seen.

Everyone around us is, as they say, beatifically stoned. The apartment is sweet with weed. As the evening wears on, gradually, clothes begin to come off. I look over my shoulder and notice that Zack is shirtless. This kind of thing isn't unusual. Parties here often end with the last few participants sitting around naked, puffing from a hookah and trying to pair off. Pretty soon, a good number of people are half-undressed, but I'm so hazy and sleepy that it doesn't really register.

I'm nearly asleep, my arm around Ruth and nestled into her back, when there's a commotion across the room. What the fuck? mumbles Zack. People are backing away from what looks like a fight. The gay kid who was flirting with James now lies on the floor, no shirt on, his mouth bloody.

It takes me a minute to notice that Ruth is gone. I'm looking around for her when I'm distracted again by tumult—James is snarling at the gay kid, looming over him with lips curled back. A few people are tentatively holding his shoulders, urging restraint.

Don't, he's snarling.

ANTOSCA

Placatory words are being whispered in his ear. Arms are tugging him back. The bloodied kid gets to his feet, wiping his mouth and grimacing, disappearing into the crowd. I turn to Zack.

What happened? Did you see it?

He shrugs. Dunno . . . with him, who knows.

Seemed pretty pissed off . . .

He's always pissed, says Zack. *Unstable* is what he is.

I look back and James is gone, too. Out of sight in a cluster of people. Then I feel a tug at my arm. Ruth has reappeared out of nowhere. With faint urgency in her voice, she says: Can we go?—and I know she's inviting me home.

We don't talk on the way back. An icy wind has started up.

Some squat animal—small dog? large cat? potbellied pig?—dashes across the street. I wonder if the homeless guy in the bus shelter is dead. But he twitches as we walk past. I suppress cold, intestinal horror—horror at being frozen, alone. I hate the cold. We pass a tomb of purplish gray stone; it is the size of a large house and has no windows. A crazy, temporally confused bird cries in the trees. I am wearing Ruth's backpack.

She lives on the top floor of Saybrook. The heat in the dorms is too high and by the time we reach her hallway, our faces are not only wind-bitten but dripping with sweat.

Her room is cramped and roasting. Paintings are smeared directly on the cream-colored walls.

Books are everywhere, open like drugged birds, and little figurines and trinkets and broken glass pipes lie all over the dresser and desk.

I glance at her bookshelf. *London Fields*, *Maldoror*, *Seduction of the Minotaur*, *Slouching Toward Bethlehem*, *Nightwood*: I'm relieved to see nothing by Virginia Woolf.

FIRES

Ruth gives a raspy cough. I am *so fucking sick*, she mutters, taking off her jacket. And *hungry*. I gotta eat.

I'm wondering what's expected of me. If I should leave or not. I'm not sure I actually want to sleep with her tonight, sick as she is. I let her backpack drop with a thud.

Where's the bathroom?

Down the hall. The one that says 'Bathroom.' You're coming back, aren't you?

Yeah. Of course.

In the bathroom, I run hot water over my red, dry hands. The numbness fades.

The warmth of the air makes me drowsy, and I am remembering a time when I was dared to keep my hand in a bucket of ice water for five minutes. Six or seven years ago at an eighth grade picnic. A day when the maples were exploding with leaves like giant, green flower buds. I lasted maybe forty seconds, trying to impress Kate something-or-other. Dimly I remember that a kid tried after me, succeeded, and went to the hospital with nerve damage. What a beautiful spring day in Maryland that was.

The water burns me, killing my nostalgia. I hurriedly dry my hands.

Back in her bedroom, the microwave is humming and Ruth is busily massaging lotion into her cheeks and throat. The crust of a hastily devoured peanut butter sandwich lies on a paper plate. Her sweater's off. She's wearing a black t-shirt, jeans and red socks. Her heart-shaped face is framed by tangles of dark hair. A contradictory face: naïve and corrupted. I find myself staring at wisps of brown hair on her arms. Why are innocent details so erotic?

I notice her hands, her long delicate fingers and pale, unpainted nails. The nails are chewed. Her snow-colored palms look vulnerable.

And yet their tiny pads of muscle, their porcelain curves, are oddly voluptuous.
   The microwave, half-hidden under a shawl in case fire inspectors drop in, beeps. She takes out two chipped mugs and pours a finger of 151 into each. A scent of hot chocolate.
   Milk products, bad for a cold, I warn.
   Oh yes, I know, she says. I would never do anything bad for me. Besides, you also shouldn't drink rum when you've been taking cold medicine.
   She gives me a mug. I smile. Her nose crimson, her ears flushed scarlet—she's adorable. I sip the hot chocolate and pretend it isn't awful. She grabs my arm and makes me sit on the bed beside her. She's playful and flirting and probably contagious, but I don't care because she's beautiful. She folds her legs under her. We press against each other and drink hot chocolate.
   Just try to pretend that it doesn't taste foul, okay?
   I've been doing that a couple minutes now, yeah.
   She raises her eyebrows. You martyr. Take your filthy, dirty, rock-salty shoes off my bed, while you're at it?
   I can do that, too, I sigh.
   I kick my shoes off and they hit the floor with a double thud. Peeling her socks off, she flexes her feet, small and bare. They are almond on top and ivory on the soles and I resist the urge to grab them, trapping them in my hands like doves. Little patches of sweat are visible in the underarms of her t-shirt. I'm sweating, too. She has a piquant, tangy smell. After a while she opens her window and we can smell the breeze.

   She kisses me.
   She warns me first. She says, If you're worried about catching what I've got, be ready to push me off you in about two seconds. Then

she sets her hot chocolate on the windowsill and leans over me and discovers my mouth.

She tastes like rum and chocolate—although there's bitterness on her tongue, the taste of her illness, soon to be *my* illness. But I don't mind. We kiss and the breeze comes in the window and her eyes stay closed.

A long kiss, but not aggressively sexual. More gentle than anything, just exploratory. After a while she sits back to look at me, eyes red-rimmed and uncertain, and I tell her, The hot chocolate tastes better in your mouth.

She should smile but she doesn't—instead, she kisses me again. While our mouths are crushed together I think about how good it feels to be with someone again.

And now we lie down and kiss more and clumsily get under the covers, tangled up and nuzzling.

Her body—after we're mostly undressed, clothes on the floor—is cold with sweat, but it's shaking a little and I can feel her heartbeat all through it. She turns off the light.

We kiss in the dark, under blankets, and suddenly she's massaging her throat and pressing her face into the pillow, coughing. It's a horrible raspy sound and I realize we're definitely not going to have sex tonight. I don't mind.

We settle down, not kissing much, just wrapped around each other. Pillows are strewn around the bed like they always are in girls' beds, but I keep accidentally knocking them on the floor. She gropes for the bedside table—leaning across me, her bra scratching my chin—and finds cough medicine. She drinks—a long gurgle in the dark—and caps the bottle. Then she presses against me. I feel warm breath on my neck and a rush of emotions and then, unexpectedly, I want to tell her all kinds of things, all my stories—and I want to learn about her, her history, all mine, now. Just who she is, what

makes her, what she loves and remembers.
 I say, I can feel your heart beating. Right here, through your bra.
 Mmf. I can feel yours against my stomach.
 Far away, behind our silence, we hear the rumble of street cleaners. Later, in the early morning, a garbage truck will make a huge, awful clanging as it empties a dumpster on the next block. And just before the dawn, athletes with burly, heedless voices on their way to practice will wake light sleepers on the lower floors. In the darkness it is all comforting.
 It's good you've got a single, I murmur. I don't have a roommate either.
 I petition the Dean's Office every year. I tell them I can't live with other people.
 I *wanted* a roommate, I tell her. But I was last in the housing draw.
 Poor you.
 I like going to sleep in other people's rooms, I murmur.
 Yeah?
 Yeah.
 You sound like a girl.
 Well, you *are* a girl.
 Mm. But I don't act like one.
 Can't outwit your hormones.
 I just repress them.
 Repress them?
 I'm a cruel and tyrannical dictator. That is, I'm on the pill.
 Yeah, but 'the pill' is still a sugar pill like, five days a month. So you *are* outwitting them, sort of.
 Seven. Seven days. As in, a week.
 Whatever.
 Don't know much about women, do you?
 Shut up.

She shivers a bit with laughter. Her body is a heavy ribbon of warmth up my side, her leg is curled over mine. I feel the cotton of her bra scratching my ribs and close my eyes and imagine what it will be like to fuck her, because I know it will happen eventually. I think I know. Yes, I know. Doesn't matter. Right now, in this moment, I'm doing all right. One of those moments.

Her body is heaving in slow, regular intervals and I wonder if she's asleep. She mutters, That, that was the . . .

What?

. . . scariest movie I've ever . . .

Shhh. You're dreaming.

Before I drift to sleep I tell myself: Be careful. Hold onto this one. Don't be stupid again.

* * *

I wake gasping. Something's near. Something huge and covered in sweat.

—and it's gone. I fight for breath. A human arm, hot and monstrous, was digging up out of my chest. I'm trembling.

Beside me, she jerks half-awake, mumbling, enfolding me in slender dark arms.

Mm. You okay?

Yeah. I had a, a dream. A nightmarish—dream.

You mean a 'nightmare'? She makes sleepy quotation marks in the air.

Yeah. Yeah, a nightmare.

But after a while, reassured by the drowsy warmth beside me, I sink into the pillow again. The window's closed now—she must have risen to do it as I slept—and I'm warm. Soon I have no difficulty getting back to sleep. No more dreams come.

ANTOSCA

It's late when we wake. In our sleep we kicked blankets off and we are splayed in awkward positions, sweaty, our legs tangled. She laughs and says that the muscles in her back hurt. The room's burning up. Hey, she says, I had a dream with you in it. We were deer. I got a salt lick.

That's a *great* dream, I say.

In the sunlight, I notice little scars on Ruth's back, like baby half-moons. What are these? I ask, and she says: How should I know, I can't see my own back. She blows her nose into a kleenex and I lean across her and shove the window open, leaning out and sucking icy air.

From four stories up I see kids scattered on the quad, in their winter jackets, breath visible. Wait, hold on. James Dearborn is there. James Dearborn is sitting on a bench and smoking. James Dearborn is disheveled and haggard, like he didn't go home from the party last night.

A girl from one of my classes looks up at me as I lean shirtless out the window, skin prickling in the cold. She waves, grinning, and I duck inside.

Let me get in the bathroom first, okay? Ruth says in a scorched voice, getting out of the bed. My own throat feels raw, sandpapery. Sun is pouring in the room. I notice fading, yellow-violet marks on Ruth's shoulders, her torso, the tops of her breasts.

Hey, what're those? I ask. Bruises?

Huh. Yeah. I bruise easily.

Ouch.

Ruth gathers her shower things. She picks something from her eye, tosses a robe over her shoulder, and leaves for the bathroom.

I lie down in the messy bed, on the sweat-damp sheets. The air is turning cold. In daylight, her room looks bigger.

FIRES

Lying here, with winter sunlight streaming in, I feel like things are right in the world. It's one of those rare, crystallized moments when by some confluence of events, life seems happy and ripe. All my doubts and fears are just hollow, flimsy things, like corn husks. Inevitably I think of home, in the summer: honey-colored light, the smell of burnt leaves, the blue splash of swimming pools, the fields where new houses grow.

When Ruth comes back, she's robed and her dark hair is wet and pulled back, and despite puffy eyes and a red nose, her face is plain and sweet.

I roll out of bed as she rubs moisturizer into her hands. Her glance—sideways, sudden—is almost shy, as if she's surprised to find me in her room. Uncertainty tugs at me; I freeze (caught! But at what?), looking at her. Her throat and upper chest are red, flushed from the shower. She cocks her head expectantly.

What? I ask.

I'm just waiting for you to go take a shower so I can change.

Oh, sorry.

Abashed, I go into the hall.

I take a gloriously hot shower, cough and spit at the drain (my throat is getting worse by the minute and I'm slightly woozy, heavy-headed), breathe steam, and wash my hair with a scented bar of soap I find in the shower. There are four different kinds of conditioner and long hairs are coiled around the drain. I turn off the water and dry myself with a pink towel, wrap it around me. The guy in the mirror needs to shave. He looks pretty pleased with himself, though.

Back in the hallway, I bump into a different girl who lives here—a redhead wrapped in a towel, all freckles and creamy skin—and hurry back to Ruth's room.

She's lying in bed in a t-shirt and panties. Sunlight makes everything gold. Ruth smiles when I come in, her hair damp and loose and spread on the pillow. She moves over to make room, covering herself with the blanket. I get under the covers with her, wearing just the towel, and she closes her eyes, not modest anymore. The kiss lasts a while.

We stay in bed all morning, into the afternoon. Nursing sore throats, commiserating. By afternoon we are both undressed, but we tease each other, not having sex yet by unspoken agreement. We drink rum and it hurts to laugh. In the late afternoon, the sun goes away and we are bathed in wistful shadows, lying side by side, happy and miserable.

Being sick

By Saturday she's better, but I'm worse. The germ has its way with me, with my skull, with all the tissues and sweet stuff in there. Like a blowtorch going through. My voice becomes a rasp, as if I'm caught in the middle of a sob.

Feeling responsible for the illness, Ruth takes care of me. I stay in my room all weekend, in bed, while she makes trips to the drugstore and brings back lozenges, orange juice, Excedrin. She takes my cigarettes away. She keeps a steady rotation of CDs in my stereo, from Wilco to The Residents to Dylan to Pavement. She finishes writing my bullshit British Novel essay for me. She cooks soup which she buys as bouillon at the grocery (botching it horribly—how is that possible?) and brings it to me in a thermos, fresh from her microwave.

I fall asleep and have nightmares where I'm back in high school (which is odd—I *liked* high school) sitting in an auditorium with my friends Ben and Russ, and James Dearborn is on stage eating an ice cream sundae while he delivers his valedictory speech, and on top of the ice cream sundae like cherries are my severed nipples, which are chewy and tough but he eats them.

Ruth sits on my bed and reads. She makes more trips to the drugstore, bringing tissues, magazines, cough medicine.

Be quiet, you sound like a tracheotomy patient, she says when I try to rasp a thanks.

Then she makes a face at me, screwing up her mouth and her dark eyes—one of those strange expressions that lay bare her contradictions, the wounded innocence, the toughness, the sense that you could hit her a thousand times and she'd get back up, but find a special cruelty and she'll recoil in terror.

By Sunday night, the pain in my throat has settled into a kind of stinging rawness. We watch TV in the common room until midnight, lying on an old sofa, and I discover I can laugh without agony. Ruth is smoking a joint and laughing that thick, genuine laugh, and her honey-colored arms are wrapped around her knees.

She sleeps over in my room, stoned and purring. I'm drowsy from the medicine and she's so out of it she doesn't wake up when I steal the sheets. My head feels stuffed with wet cotton. I can hardly breathe. My throat is still raw.

All in all, I'm happy.

<u>Night</u>

I FOLLOW A YOUNG, half-naked man across the grass into a weird wall of rain, afraid for some reason he will be hit by a car.

Half-built houses are visible in the feverish rain. Boxy plasterboard skeletons, plastic-draped ghosts. Hundreds of them. Thousands. The sound of warm rain on wood and plastic is amplified, erotic.

I follow him across soft fields in my bare feet. Past doghouses like children's crypts. Past great dark holes—the graves of giant men—where swimming pools will soon be. Past swing sets like little gallows.

Wrinkled, wet fast-food wrappers are everywhere, tumbling like drunken moths across the grass, although there's no wind to blow them.

I follow him across wet dark asphalt. We drift across a lawn, and he stops. I stop. We stand before a skeleton of a house, its plasterboard bones cloaked in sheets of translucent gray plastic.

It is my house.

When he turns to look back, I see that he's my age. Rain blurs his face and his sinewy arms glisten with trickling water. I feel bruised, like someone has been beating me, or hugging me too hard.

Go in, I urge. Go in my house.

He is still looking back at me. I am naked.

* * *

I wake and brush the dream away. Beside me, Ruth stirs.
I had a dream about you, I murmur.

Recovery

BY MONDAY MORNING, I'm better. The sore throat has subsided. Ruth is asleep in one of my old t-shirts and a pair of boxers. I study her doe-brown, alien face (eyes closed, long dark lashes twitching) and remember her from last night, lovely and stoned.

I take a hot shower, breathing steam to loosen gunk in my throat, and when I come back, she's awake. Half-dressed, bare-legged, pulling socks over her beige feet.

I've got Gaddis in forty minutes, she says. I have to pick up my books, so I'll just take a shower at my suite. You're looking better.

I am, I say, getting into bed and throwing the towel aside. Thanks for, you know, everything. That was really something.

No problem, she says. I like taking care of people.

You're good at it.

Thank you!

She grins her innocent, corrupted grin and wriggles a pair of jeans over her hips. I reach out to grab her leg and she dodges playfully, then bends down to leave a quick kiss on my arm.

After she's gone, I linger in bed, sucking on a lozenge and staring at the ceiling. The taste of the lozenge reminds me of sick days as a kid. I think about home, my neighborhood in Maryland, the Appalachians looming over us, Bondurant High with its burgundy and gold colors and its Bondurant Bonfire. Burning leaves. The smell of chlorine from the public pool.

I cough. I want coffee and a cigarette.

After a while I rise and drift into the common room, bare feet picking up crumbs from the old rug. None of the other guys are around, which is fine with me.

Sun pours into the common room, and the big elm shakes its branches outside the window. I turn the TV on and leave the volume low. Children's cartoons sing to me. I flip channels, thinking about the last few days. They're like fever dreams. Too hard to hold under the light, too fragile and weird.

So I lie in the sun-drenched common room with the elm tree quietly shaking its limbs by the window, and I watch a kids' program. A toy train winds along under a green mountain range. A fake orange sun with cheerful little flames around its perimeter blazes surreally an inch above the mountains. Then puppets dance.

I'm sitting on the green. Thinking and watching as the sun sets. I'm watching people walk by, walking dogs, talking, smoking. I see a freshman I slept with last month walking with her new boyfriend. The twilight light is murky, like the middle depths of an ocean.

After dark, I walk over to Ruth's. I find her room empty but unlocked, so I go inside to wait. Its messiness fascinates me; it must be what the inside of her mind looks like.

But by now it's past midnight. I lie in bed, waiting. I try to read *Maldoror*, but fall asleep. A dream of smoke and crows segues into semi-conscious darkness, and after a time I feel the warmth of a body against mine. I make dumb sleep noises as I put my arms around her.

Good to find you here, she whispers, her voice strange. I nuzzle her breasts. She digs her fingers into my spine and makes a purring, growling sound. She smells like liquor and girl sweat. Toothpaste on her breath.

You smell good.

Give me some more covers. I want to get under with you.

Take some. Where were you?

Put your arm under my neck and I'll lie like this.

'Kay.

I'm going to sleep. Kiss me.

I do. We settle our heads into the pillow. Her breathing trembles and slows. Sound carries at night, and I hear a drunk girl sobbing. A breeze comes in the window and after a while I try to sleep. But my nerves are too sensitive to Ruth's presence, attuned to her noises and tremblings. A few moments pass, or perhaps an hour. Finally, I shake her.

You awake? I ask, trying to wake her. You still awake, Ruth?

Little. A little.

Wake up. Are you dreaming?

Her eyes are closed, but I can tell she's awake. I watch thick, dappled shadows on her face. The branches rustle outside the window.

What were you dreaming about?

FIRES

Nothing.

Tell me.

Mm. No.

Then tell me something. Tell me about your friends. Your life. Tell me things.

Mm, she says. Boring stuff.

Just tell me things. About you. Tell me something.

Everybody has the same stories.

Come on. I want to know more about you.

Jesus Christ, Jon, shut up. It's the middle of the fucking night and I'm cold and I just want to feel you next to me. So just shut up and hold me or something.

All right, okay.

Press against me. I want to be warm.

You're sweating.

My front is hot but my back is cold.

It's nice.

You've been keeping me awake, you fuck. Now I'm thirsty again.

There was a bottle of apple juice—I saw it on the desk maybe—

I flick on the lamp and lean across her toward the desk, blinking in the light—then stop. Her breasts and neck are covered in bruises. She knows I've seen them and seems to shrink away from me.

What is this?

I bruise easily.

Her arms fold to cover the markings.

Ruth, those are finger marks.

Turn off the light.

What happened? Who did this?

Please turn the light off.

Taking her by the wrists, I unwrap her arms from her chest and press them to the bed. The bruises are red and fresh, still forming.

Ruth, who did this?

I can't, she says. I can't. Please. Turn the light off.

Tell me.

She turns her face to the side and closes her eyes. I will once you turn it off.

Releasing her wrists, I reach for the lamp and flick it off. Again we're steeped in darkness, and the bruises become steel-colored smudges, hard to see. Shadows.

Who hurt you?

She nuzzles her head into the pillow as if trying to get away, but I am lying on top of her and she can't turn her body away from me.

I'll tell you what I can tell you, she says. But make me a promise.

What?

Don't push me to tell you more.

I can't promise that.

If you don't, it's over now, whatever's between us. Don't make this worse for me. I swear it'll be over, like that.

I look into the darkness that masks her face and feel my rage turn to fear. All right, I say. Tell me.

She wriggles out from under me and sits up on her elbows. Before you I was with someone else, she says. I should have got out of it a long time ago but I didn't know how and I wasn't sure what I wanted. Tonight I saw him and I told him it was over, for real this time.

He did this to you?

I—it's not his fault.

He did it?

No. Yes. Sort of. It's different than what you're thinking.

Did he rape you? Tonight? Some time?

No. He didn't.

I lean my face in to where my eyes are just inches from hers, intensely close.

Who is he?

You promised.

Who?

I'm not going to tell you his name. I'm with you now and it'll be okay. It doesn't matter about anybody else.

He goes here?

She pauses, hesitating. No. He's not a student here.

Ruth, I slowly say, give me his name.

No. If you want to help me, then just be with me and don't ask questions. It's the past, and it's over, and anyway it was nothing.

Listen to me, Ruth—

A faint note of hysteria comes into her voice. If you're going to be a jerk, then get out. Take it or leave it, but don't break your promises.

For a few moments I lapse into silence, furious (and jealous), my breath coming fast. Hers too. Then she softens and encircles me with her arms. I can feel the muscles trembling.

Hold me, she says. Just hold me. No questions.

Your heart is going really fast, I say, listening, allowing her to lay my head between her breasts.

Hold me and we'll go to sleep, she says.

* * *

My arm's dead. Pins and needles; radiating pain. Trying not to wake Ruth, I drag my arm out from under her. The nightmare—the nightmare. I catch my breath.

I remember more of this one. Things were happening . . . someone pulled out my teeth and fed them to me . . . the campus was divided into warring tribes, and legacies drank the blood of financial aid students . . . alumni mated with St. Bernards . . . I went home to Maryland, where it was balmy, and people I knew from high school were there.

In the darkness I look over at Ruth and try to make out the bruises. We still haven't had sex.

voice

WE'VE ALMOST FINISHED our lunch at Samurai when Ruth leaves for the bathroom. A waiter walks past, delivering a hissing, smoky platter to a nearby table, and, using chopsticks, I bathe the last piece of my dragon roll in soy sauce and pop it in my mouth. I pick bits of ginger off my plate and eat them.

There is a subtle buzzing. Ruth's purse. It's on the floor, half-open and trembling—and I can see the black nose of her cell phone poking out. After a moment of hesitation, I reach into her purse and, with a twinge of guilt, take out the phone. It could be something important, I tell myself.

PRESS ANY is flashing below the words PRIVATE NUMBER, so I press a button, put the phone to my ear, and say—

Hello?

Yeah? Who's this? (A male voice, surprised.)

I ask, Who's *this*?

I dialed 203-436-4650.

That's right.

Where's Ruth? This is Ruth's number.

Not here right now.

Where is she?

She's busy. Give me your name, I'll let her know you called.

There is a short pause, punctuated by a soft growl, and then he hangs up.

I set the phone down. After a moment, though, I pick it up again, go to the RECEIVED CALLS log, and scroll down to the most recent number. It says PRIVATE. No number logged. I place the phone conspicuously on top of her napkin.

As I wait for her to return, I stab at the wet towel beside my plate with a chopstick. I should have said something. Should have asked—are you the one? Did you hurt her? Should have told him that if I ever find out who he is I'll beat him until his testicles withdraw into his body. But now uncertainty gets me, because I hardly know any of Ruth's friends, and she must have male friends, and—but she comes back in, dodging a blank-faced waiter, and sits down, not noticing the displacement of her phone.

The check? she asks.

Your phone rang. I answered it.

You did? Who was it?

It was a guy. He wouldn't give his name.

Her hands pause in the act of rearranging her napkin. She cocks her head.

What else did he say?

Nothing. He wanted to know who I was.

What'd you tell him?

Nothing. Any idea who it might have been?

A wrong number? Why did you answer my phone? You shouldn't have done that.

He asked for you by name. Was it him, Ruth?

Who?

You know who.

She gives me a hard, piercing look, her mouth set. No. It wasn't.

How do you know?

Well—she hesitates, then says unconvincingly—I never let him have my cell number.

Her manner turns suddenly into a parody of distracted casualness, and she busies herself with brushing tempura crumbs out of her napkin.

Dolls, Love

It's hard to comprehend, sometimes, how easy and natural the afternoons feel when I spend them with her.

We're in her room. Blue shadows paint the walls. For a while we lie beside each other on the bed, not talking. The curves at the sides of her mouth seem mischievous, but her eyes are innocent, and when she looks at me with an offer in them, I silently accept. We kiss, staying on top of the blankets, and pale light is coming into the room. Her t-shirt's off, but otherwise we're fully dressed. Her nipples are stiff against her blue cotton bra.

I start to unbutton her jeans but she says, Let me. So I'm kissing her stomach as she pulls them down her hips, showing white underwear with little blue leaves. I bite her nipples a little through her bra and when she digs into my wrist with her nails, I get the message—*harder*. We kiss for a while longer and I feel vibrations in her chest, a purr; she's trembling.

Hurt me, she says, hit me.

I'm not sure if she's serious, if she actually wants pain, or if it's just something she likes to say. So I dig my fingernails first tentatively, then fiercely, into her hips.

She arches her body to let my hands under her; my fingers outsmart the tiny hooks of her bra and it lands on the floor. Her nipples are small, hard, and dark brown. I fumble with my belt as she slides her panties past her knees, kicks them away. Then I have my jeans off, boxers with them. There are condoms on her desk and I tear one open. I try to put it on, too hastily—

FIRES

Wrong *way*, she says, laughing.

I *know*, I reply, turning it around to unroll it the right way.

Then she lunges up to bite my shoulder and drags her nails across my back, probably drawing blood, and pushes her hips up toward mine, opening her legs. I push inside of her, slowly, feel her thighs grab my hipbones, feel her clenched teeth pressing into my neck. Slow, she commands, just go slow for a minute. So I do, inching deeper a little at a time, pushing her down on the bed so we're looking into each other's eyes, and her pupils have dilated—they're huge, like black coins, her irises nothing but thin brown outlines. Slow, she says, gritting her teeth. Her breath comes out in little snarling whimpers, her lips are pulled back. Then I'm all the way inside her, she's clenching me, and she snarls excitedly in my ear,

Now—come on, *hurt* me.

Later, when my muscles ache and the teethmarks, about which I feel sort of guilty, are becoming bruises on her wrists, shoulders, chest, and almost everywhere else, she opens a window to let in cold air and we get under the blankets. We press against each other, wedded in sweat. I have sick-sweet lubricant on my fingers. She rolls sideways, wincing, and kisses me.

My back hurts, she says.

Sorry.

It's okay. It'll go away.

Want me to do something? Rub it?

No, it'll go away.

But I rub her back a little anyway, with one aching hand. Then we lie there, in silence, in the shadows. Cold air mixes with stale dormitory air and I feel her shivering.

I trace my fingers along her bare side, touching, exploring. I touch her ribs, her waist, the curve of her ass. Her body is ferociously warm.

My fingers rest on the velvety bud of her nipple, then travel over her breast to tease her armpit, with its small sharp hairs nestled in soft flesh.

Tell me, I say. Tell me about you.

What do you want to know? she murmurs.

About you. About your life.

Boring stuff.

Come on.

It's all the same.

Nuzzling her neck, I whisper in her ear. Fine, I say. You have no history.

The shadows deepen and turn the color of the sea. It sounds like birds are fighting in the elm tree, and we can hear people outside. I think about how good it feels to be lying here naked, still suspended in the stickiness of sex, listening to the oblivious world.

I played with dolls, she laughs softly. Barbies. That's one thing.

Every girl did, right?

That's my point. (She pauses.) Actually, uh, no. I don't think I played with them the way other girls did.

Yeah?

Yeah. Like, I had *hundreds* of Barbies. An army of them. It's funny because I'm not that kind of girl, right? The kind you would think of as playing with dolls as a kid? But from about six years old until—almost *ten*, actually—I lived this like fantasy life through Barbie, making her live out these, like, rigid routines. Nothing even remotely interesting or adventurous, just, like, Barbie goes to the store and gets a ham, and then comes home and cooks the ham, and then does a hundred crunches, and then Ken comes home and they sleep on top of the covers. And every few weeks she'd have a baby.

Exciting.

No, it was like, maybe I'm not describing how demented it was.

How necessary it felt to me to have this routine for Barbie. I don't think other girls were doing this sort of thing.

What were other girls doing?

Well, you know, taking their clothes off and rubbing them together, stuff like that. Not me, though. For me it was about imagining a normal life.

What'd you do with all of them? All those dolls, I mean.

Eventually? Well, buried them, actually. Buried them. There's a mass grave of Barbies under our bird feeder.

That's weird.

I know. So. Now you know something about me. Happy now?

You smell good.

Really? What do I smell like?

Kind of—biscuity. And like pine.

I use a man's deodorant.

And like spice, a little.

I don't know why that is.

She goes silent. We rest in the shadows, listening to the distant, muted sounds of the city. Students walking home from class, taxis barking at each other, police sirens crying. After a little while, I close the windows.

I say, It's nice with the light off.

Mmm, I know.

Usually I hate the dark.

I love it. I want to go to Alaska after the sun sets there.

Ruth wriggles up a little, presses her forehead into my collarbone.

I used to sleep with all the lights on, I tell her. When I was a kid.

I love the dark. You know, when I was nine I ran away from home.

Yeah?

But instead of running, you know, I just went two blocks down. The neighbors had sold the place and moved out. The new people weren't going to be there for a couple weeks.

Turning sideways, she throws an arm over me, her breasts crushing up against my waist.

Why'd you run away?

In the house where I hid there were no lights. The fuses, something. I lived on the second floor. I was alone. Eventually I got worried about my brother and went back home, but by the time I did, I'd lost six pounds, which, I mean, for a little kid that's a lot. I never got scared, though, not once, being alone in the dark for so long.

I remain silent, baffled.

I ask—You have a brother?

She says, Let's sleep.

A week later, we are drinking rum at night on the New Haven green. The air is chilly—we can see our breath even when it isn't mixed with cigarette smoke. A blue, dirt-caked teddy bear lies in the grass. Ruth's wearing wool mittens. The night sky is clear, the stars like diamonds scattered on black marble. And she says—

How do you feel now?

Um . . . fine.

A black-eyed squirrel darts erratically across the grass. Is it rabid? Do they get rabies?

Why? Why do you ask?

No reason.

Oh.

Silence again; the night air seeps into my veins, my blood. She doesn't usually play conversational hide-and-seek. Something's up. I exhale a phantom of warm breath, watching it dissipate. I say—

Why? How do *you* feel right now?

I don't know. I think . . .

What?

She sighs. I think. I think I'm getting attached to you.

FIRES

I don't say anything. A UFO darts across the night sky. My fingers are numb even inside new gloves. Moments pass and the elms breathe all around us in the winter darkness. I drink some rum, feel it feed the torch in my chest. Ruth sighs again.

Aren't you going to say anything? she murmurs with disappointment. I can almost hear bruises forming. I say,

I love you.

I hear—and see—all the breath come out of her lungs. She leans against me and then she turns and kisses me sloppily under the ear. She's shivering. Her brown eyes are large and wet, glistening in the darkness. For a moment her face has no contradictions at all.

Do I love her? A few weeks ago, we didn't even know each other—the idea's ridiculous. Or maybe not. Because I have this desire, a need to be around her all the time and touch her and penetrate her. And I find her strange, alien beauty more fascinating every day. But am I in love? Am I even capable of love? Or am I—and this seems, in fact, disturbingly plausible—in love with the idea of her?

Well, the idea of not being alone.

In the icy darkness I chew my lip, wondering with shaken nerves what I've committed too. I wonder whether I have the right to make a commitment, whether I have the intestinal fortitude, the strength of character, to stick my hand in that flame and keep it there. I'm not too sure. So I say it again.

Ruth, I love you.

She's leaning against me, the weight of her body powerful and erotic. Her hair is tangled with shadows. Her face, from the side, looks almost Arabic. A freezing squirrel, fur in jagged tufts, watches us. A jetliner scrapes a thin white line across the frozen sky.

So we shiver together in the darkness, and it's possible I've lied. I feel guilty, exhilarated. Horrified at the lie—if it was a lie. Because maybe I *do* love her. Maybe I was right to put my hand in this flame.

After that we are inseparable. My secret doubts in the park notwithstanding, I am obsessed. Desire this humbling and complete is new to me.

Weeks pass, winter fades. I see the sun rise through her window. We stay awake and fuck until breakfast. Then we sleep. I have nightmares from time to time and wonder how long this can last before it falls apart. We don't go to class much anymore.

speaking softly

THE FIRST TIME I TOLD A GIRL I LOVED HER, I didn't have any doubts. It was only that clueless, dumb, sweet feeling that gets drunk on itself and idealizes. But still it was nice.

My high school girlfriend and I went to her cousin's house in Fairfax most weekends because her uncle had a bar in his house and a big swimming pool. The cousin was twelve or thirteen, shy, and didn't bother us much. One evening as an orange sun was setting, we sat by the edge of the water in deck chairs and dangled our feet, watching the sunset play on the pool like wet flames.

She wore a one-piece bathing suit, navy blue, and in the subsiding heat it was nearly dry. Her sunburn was peeling. She was tall and her long white feet dipped into the pool.

I watched the sunset throb on the water, and it seemed to draw something forth from me; its boldness and color had an epic feel, like a biblical flood or a lightning storm. It was as though shards of the sun had been tossed down to float, quivering, on the water. The sun sank lower and the shards turned red, like blood on a griddle.

My own blood seemed alive, full of thrilling drugs (I remembered getting high with James Dearborn, sheets of wet plastic flapping

FIRES

around us like the raincoats of ghosts) and I tilted my head toward Sara.

I love you, I whispered very quietly.

So quietly that, to my relief, she didn't seem to hear and never took her eyes from the mesmerizing crimson water. I looked away, savoring the blissful warmth in my chest that came from saying those words, and also glad that she had not heard and therefore could not later use it against me.

spring

Bondurant, Maryland, pop. 3,500. It's a nice place. There's a high school, a public library, a volunteer fire station, a shopping center with grocery store and beauty salon. Long streets with maple trees. I live in a subdivision just outside of Bondurant. The place is Copper Creek Estates, a cluster of several hundred homes like a colony of cheerful mushrooms at the foot of the Appalachian Mountains.

It is summer in Bondurant and I am thirteen. I am on the swim team, flirting with girl swimmers in their green, sleek swimsuits.

Thirteen, fourteen. I take piano lessons. I mow neighbors' lawns for five dollars each during the summer, ten as I get older. The guy across the street, the football coach, pays to have his lawn cut every Sunday. Afterward, he comes out on the porch with iced coffee and pays, and I feel pleasant and tired as I drink the coffee and listen to him talk about—I don't remember.

Fifteen, sixteen. I play soccer and volunteer at the library. I walk through the pouring rain one night with James Dearborn, who is exuberant and dangerous. I smoke weed with RJ and Ben on the bleachers some evenings and smile at local cops when I see them around. Everybody knows everybody and they know I'm okay.

We're all the sums of our histories. The places we've lived, the people we've known, the things we've possessed and lost. We're made out of those things, with wild cards. You can sometimes look back on your life and see what you're made out of, figure out where parts of you come from—and for me, all those parts come from one place.

And Bondurant was the perfect place to grow up. It was the quintessential American town, healthy and normal, and I am as much a product of it as I am of my own parents. If any further evidence is needed of my hometown's benevolence and communal vigor, consider this: although I was an only child with two working parents, I have almost no memory of ever being alone.

* * *

I'm on a bench outside Harkness, smoking after class. Zack Roper is here with me, eating yellow rice and chicken that he bought from the vendor on Chapel. It is steaming and smells like curry. The weather's warmer and I'm wearing a light sweater. Two stringy-tailed squirrels screech and tussle on the grass; other squirrels look on.

They should feed squirrels to the homeless, Zack opines.

I blow smoke and reply, Someone was saying the other day on C-SPAN that they're going to feed the homeless to squirrels.

Shit, I took this summer program at Duke when I was in high school, and they had all these, like, Korean kids there. (He forks a heap of rice into his mouth.) Some of them didn't speak the English too good. Most, it was their first time in America. This one skinny guy would stand at my window, like, staring at the squirrels—because they were *everywhere*—and he'd jab his finger and go like, 'Weaser!, Weaser!'

Weaser?

Weasel.

I laugh. Zack picks something rubbery out of his rice and tosses it on the grass. A creature that looks like a black squirrel crossed with a toad gets to the food first. I play with a book of matches, watching kids flow in and out of Harkness.

Zack says, So you're, like, married now?

Well, I mean—yeah, it's getting serious.

We never see you anymore.

Look at that squirrel.

So what's the deal?

What's the deal? I'm with *her*.

I know that. (He scrapes yellow rice off the styrofoam container. Squirrels natter and poke where he threw the piece of gristle. The monster squirrel is gone.) But it's serious? he asks.

You going deaf? Yeah, it's serious.

I'm just saying.

You sound really enthusiastic about the success of our relationship.

Oh, I am.

He picks at the curried chicken with his plastic fork. More squirrels gather—a congregation has formed where Zack is throwing the food. Some fight peevishly. There are a dozen, at least. I toss a half-burned match on the grass and they examine it, disdainful.

I'm just saying, Zack repeats.

What are you saying?

I'm saying I hear things.

Things?

You know, things like, 'That girl's crazy' or 'She gets around' or 'She smokes crack.' You know, things.

Who said she smokes crack?

I made that up. But the others I hear.

What? That she cheated on me? You heard that?

No, no, I didn't say that. I just heard, yeah, she gets around. Like, before you, I mean. She got with a lot of guys. I'm not trying to insult you. I'm just saying what I heard.

The memory of her bruised throat and breasts comes back to me. It has been a while, perhaps longer than a week, since I've thought of it. It seems like a nauseous dream, hard to accept, hard to reconcile with day-to-day life.

Like who? Who was she with?

Zack doesn't look at me. I don't know, he says. I just heard a lot of guys.

She hasn't cheated on me, I say. (Is my voice too insistent?) There hasn't been a *time* to. And she wouldn't, anyway.

Zack nods. I believe that.

I trust her.

Good for you. Excuse me a moment.

He gets to his feet and sets the styrofoam box on the bench. Then he rushes at the squirrels, waving his arms and whooping as they scatter in an explosion of dirty gray bodies, screeching in incensed little voices.

Winter segues into spring. Ruth, who is majoring in Comp Lit, works ten hours a week in the stacks, shelving and cataloging—but otherwise we spend all our time together. I put what Zack told me out of my head.

Time passes easily. The days go by in long lazy ribbons of cigarette smoke and sex and snatches of sleep. She has a tiny, black mole on the small of her back that I love to press with one fingertip. I am happy.

My professors aren't happy with me—I sleep through every class that I actually attend, barely hand in my work on time, and don't go to section—but fuck it. I'm a Humanities major, which basically means I never do any real work or thinking. And major aside, I'd have no reason to worry. Grade inflation makes it impossible to get anything lower than a C.

That feeling I used to get, that creeping feeling of emotional claustrophobia, the fear of being alone—it comes less and less.

The weather turns warmer. Memories of winter are erased by a warm March. Squirrels congregate on every possible patch of grass, shredding each other's ears over pizza crust and burying acorns only to dig them up thirty seconds later, clutch them possessively, then bury them again six inches to the left. The faces of the homeless appear less chapped and desperate. Seagulls roll in the sky, following the breeze inland from the coast, and starlings peck at sidewalk crumbs. The trees sprout buds.

I'm so fucking hungry.

You just ate, like, two hours ago.

She rolls onto her back, nude, holding her stomach. I *am*, she moans, laughing. And I get bitchy when I don't eat. Didn't you hear my stomach gurgling?

It's night, and her lamp is off, but the room is blue-silver with moonlight and the air smells like sex. *Pussy air*, she calls it—the heavy, sweaty tang that stays.

She pouts and sucks in her belly to make herself look starved.

Go buy me some Nutella.

You go buy *me* some Nutella. It's disgusting to watch you eat that stuff with your fingers, anyway. Why do girls do that?

She laughs, and there is a silvery pause. The shadows of leaves rustle on the wall.

She says, There's a lake in Easton where you can catch frogs. We should go.

Frogs? What?

We could go swimming.

Hey. I got an idea. (I stroke her bare foot with mine.) Come to the beach with me.

What, this weekend?

No, I mean spring break.

God, no. You kidding? It's cold. The pebbles hurt my feet.

Not the beach in Connecticut. My grandmother lives in Atlantic City, she has a condo like two blocks from the beach. We could stay for a week or so. Yeah?

Ruth hesitates for a moment. I dunno—maybe. Is your grandma cool? I wouldn't have to like, sleep by myself locked in the guest room?

No. She's half-blind and she can't go upstairs since her hip surgery. She'll probably think you're a boy.

Oh, thanks.

No problem.

An insectile buzzing on the bedside table startles us. Ruth reaches for her cell phone, pauses for a moment, staring at it and thinking—then turns it off. I am relieved.

Would your parents be there? she asks.

Nah. That would dredge up some alarming memories for my mother.

She smiles, seeing my face, and digs a finger into my ribs—Tell me.

Okay. So in like eleventh grade I had this girlfriend, Sara. So I convinced my mom to let her come with us to the beach for a week. But my mom was paranoid. If we even sat together on the sofa, my mom would just *glare*. It was hell. So my grandma went to evening services one night—I think it was Saturday—and my mother was upstairs taking a nap. Me and Sara went in the kitchen and started making out, and eventually she was jerking me off. That was when my mom walked in. Right at the, uh—the worst possible moment. She said something about life being over.

I can *imagine*, she laughs. Did your grandmother ever find out?

No.
Thank *god*.
Yeah, I murmur nostalgically. Sara was cool, but we never—
Oh no. No.
What?
No ex-girlfriend information. That story gets a pass, but no more. I *don't* want to know your sexual history, a list of your ex-lovers, *any* of that stuff beyond what I already know. I hate that kind of stuff. It's so insultingly unimportant. Okay?
Okay, okay.
No ex-lover information. From either of us. Agreed?
Fine! Agreed.
That *was* a great story, though.

I don't move, thinking of the fresh red bruises on her throat.

But the silence that follows is broken by her giggling, and the thought slips gratefully away. Her voice is beautiful and dark and strange. I take a cigarette from the almost-empty pack on the windowsill. Silvery light drips through her hair and she frowns.

Please. *Make* my room smell like secondhand smoke.
You smell like *firsthand* smoke, I tell her as I light the cigarette.
I smell of sugar. Perhaps also spice.
And Kamel Reds.
Look, just go out and get us something to eat, okay? Peanut butter cookies? Miso soup? Anything. I just don't want to get dressed.

I don't want to either. What happened to that other box of cookies? (I look around; the box is a dark, crushed shape in the trash can.) Never mind. Well, just find something that's already here to eat. Hey, don't fucking bite.

Then *you* bite *me*, she demands.

Restless

THE NIGHTS ARE UNSEASONABLY WARM. By the beginning of April we're wearing short sleeves and sandals every day, and it's obvious that summer's going to be a horror. Ruth tans easily, her already honey-colored arms turning a healthy copper. We study, we smoke, we drink liquor in bed, we leave marks on each other.

Sometimes she asks to be slapped, or struck, or held down and fucked, which I am learning to like more and more. It is as if she's training me, easing me into it, and I have never been with a girl this intent on being hurt before.

One night she's working overtime, helping catalog a private library that was in the national news when it was donated to Beinecke. I wander alone across campus in the gathering dusk. A group of freshmen poke at a dying fruit bat. A sense of unease, of aloneness, begins to creep over me. With relief, I encounter a guy from one of my classes sitting on a bench. I can't remember his name, but he's drunk and it doesn't matter. Somehow, we end up at a release party for a student publication.

There I find myself isolated in a sea of assholes. Yes, a sea of assholes. Apparently they run the Literary Magazine, but they seem mostly interested in wearing scarves and eating brie. My classmate has disappeared. More wine calms me a little, but soon I feel myself getting uncontrollably edgy. I head for the door.

Someone grabs my arm. A student councilman, Jeremy something. We lived together freshman year. He read self-help books because he was a sociopath and needed to learn how human beings behave.

He makes small talk. It is a transparent pretext but I don't know for what. Finally he says—Hey, man, so, I hear you two are getting serious, huh?

Me and Ruth? Yeah.

FIRES

Ruth is such a great girl—I love her, man. She has so many interesting things to say.

Yes, she does.

His introduction of Ruth into the conversation triggers something in me; I feel like a trapped animal. I manage, barely, to hide my anger.

Ruth is a great girl, he says again.

I have to go.

Tell her I said hi, man.

Why don't you tell her yourself?

Hey, hey, he says. Whoa, you seem touchy. Are you touchy? Oh, are things not working out or something? A rough patch? It'd be a shame if you broke up, man, you don't want to lose a girl like that. I'll tell you something, the time I was with her? The great part wasn't the *night*—I mean, that *was* great, don't get me wrong, she's a three-time all-star, no question—the great part was the *morning*. When I woke up she did something no girl's ever done for me. She did something that blew my mind. You know what she did? *She made me pancakes.* On a little stove in her common room. I couldn't believe it!

Instead of ripping out his larynx, I walk away. Glad I don't have a pocketknife on me. I dig out a pack of cigarettes and light one before I get to the door. Some fucker with a scarf points at me, bristling.

Hey man, we can't smoke in here.

I walk back to the drinks table and drop my cigarette in the punch bowl, where it hisses and dies. Then I slam the scowling guy full in the chest with my elbow as I walk past him to go outside.

It's dark. No one follows me or I'd probably get in a fight. I walk around in the gloom, chewing my lip, unaccountably nervous, feeling something flicker out in my chest. Finally I sit down on a bench and let the anger seep out of me until I'm just slumped and tired.

I'm walking across central campus, dodging frisbees. The heat is appalling and it's only the first week of April. Sweat stings my eyes. Here is James Dearborn coming from the opposite direction, alone. A long-sleeved black t-shirt clings to his arms, sweat-damp, and a baseball cap hides his eyes. We nod at each other. I see him a lot lately. He is always there in the distance, somehow.

I head over to the coffee shop, where Ruth waits, and we pour rum into our iced cappuccinos and drink them in the air conditioning.

James, Bondurant

I AM SIXTEEN AND A SOPHOMORE; James is a year older, a junior. I have no car. I'm skinny.

Our quarterback and a member of the National Honor Society, James has been railroaded into representing Bondurant High at a board meeting where athletic funding will be discussed. I am supposed to cover it for the school paper. That's why, at sunset, James and I are waiting for a bus in front of the high school. His license has just been suspended for reckless driving or he would have driven us there. The bus was supposed to drop us off at the meeting on its way to pick up the soccer team from scrimmage. But the bus driver seems to have forgotten.

Well, that's a bitch, James laughs as twilight settles around us. His voice is boyish, almost.

It is intimidating, how confident and handsome he is. He is only a little taller than me, but he has the presence and physique of an actor. His blond hair is short but tangled, and I notice his hands, how sculpted and veined they are. We haven't talked much, sitting here; the empty parking lot and orange-gray sky that stretch out above us seem to mute all conversation. Even to me, someone who has known him, to a greater or lesser degree, for more than ten years, his personality is unpredictable; he puts on different faces for different people and is convincing in all of them. He is one of the most popular, fascinating kids in Bondurant. I, on the other hand, am awkward and withdrawn, and will be until I go to college.

A warm drizzle comes in from the east and makes the bleachers sing distantly. Rain starts falling at our feet.

Shit, James says. Drops tap the ledge overhead. He gets to his feet and declares, I'll go inside and call my parents. You want a ride?

Yeah. Nobody's home at my house yet.

Lemme have some change.

Yeah, I got dimes and nickels. Here . . .

But when he returns from the pay phone, he is laughing. He says, Guess we gotta walk home in this.

It's not so bad.

Maybe it'll die down, he murmurs, sitting beside me again. We listen to the rain. I glance at him; he isn't smiling but looks on the verge of it.

It's not dying down, I say.

Are you gonna fucking melt?

No.

Yeah, me either. Let's go.

We start across the parking lot. In instants we are soaked. The downpour is bruising. Visibility decreases. It is like being inside a fog that hurts you.

Heads bent, shoulders hunched, we walk onto the main road. At once, two ghostly wet eyes are hurtling toward us with eerie smoothness through the rain. I react with an involuntary backward leap—my shoes scrape gravel—but James's drenched, dark figure leaps into the path of the oncoming car, waving its arms. I hear a noise like wild laughter. Then the frantic bleat of a car horn, the squeal of swerving rubber, and the angry acceleration of the car as its ghostly lights fade away, leaving James drenched and adrenalized on the yellow line.

Come on, man! he urges, hair plastered to his face.

Soaked to the bone, I hurry after. His personality—that weirdly affable menace—is magnetic, and I feel lucky to be tagging along. Twilight deepens.

The ground, loosened by rainfall, slips from under our feet in great sheets of mud as we stumble down an embankment after crossing the access road. Sulky clouds belch with thunder, and our feet sink into the farting mud as we trudge across a field where snakes are known to live. Still, there's something peaceful about the landscape, even in the rain. We traipse through neighborhoods and backyards, seeing rain turn the surfaces of swimming pools blurry. A weather-dark twilight becomes authentic night.

There are a lot of things I want to say as we walk. I want to ask James about Amanda Willoughby, a girl I heard he got with. I am still a virgin, nothing in the social universe of Bondurant High, and James, as I've said, is one of the major planets. It isn't just his athleticism or even his beauty; he has that mercurial charisma, tempered by a kind of unconscious moral innocence, that makes people want his confidence. So instead of asking about Amanda Willoughby (who I've always liked but, as it turns out, will never have a single conversation with), I yell:

Did you like the party at Brody's?

What, you were there?

No. I, I just heard about it.

It was pretty fucking cool. We smoked mad good weed. You like to puff?

Yeah, I say, sometimes.

Horseshit, he laughs. You never smoked.

Yeah I have, man. I smoked up at Jay's party, in September. *You* were there.

He laughs, and his laugh is a dangerous, knife-like thing, fierce enough to be heard above the rain. Wet hair sticks to his forehead like slashes of copper.

I *know*, man, I'm just busting your balls. Let's get high, man. Now?

At my *house*, man. It's empty.

I shrug my assent, concealing excitement. We are only a block or two from James's house. But when we reach his driveway, creamy light is glowing in the windows.

They *are* home, I say with disappointment.

No problem, I'll just pick up the shit from my room. I know another place, man. Wait in the garage, I'll be back in like two seconds.

Shivering in the darkness of the garage, I wait for James to return. Paint cans, streaked and crusty, are stacked against exposed insulation in the wall. He comes back by way of a door between the garage and kitchen; I glimpse oven mitts, oak cabinets, a cozy glow. I haven't been inside that house since a birthday party in sixth or seventh grade.

Let's go, he says. It's close.

Coughing, I follow him back into the rain. He didn't bother to pick up an umbrella or jacket at his house. Three streets over, where the neighborhood turns into sold-but-undeveloped plots of tall grass, we approach the skeleton of a house. It is draped in sheets of barely translucent, placental gray plastic—I think of embryos, things half-formed and curled in sacs—and the lawn is a brown swamp because grass seed is only just beginning to sprout. A dark-green portable toilet has been erected in the side yard. Burger King wrappers discarded by workmen lie soaked and flattened on the dirt.

Once we're in there nobody can see us, James shouts at me above the drumming rain. His tone suggests a comprehensive knowledge of drug-taking hideouts. I am suitably impressed.

    He pulls one sheet of waxy plastic aside and we step inside, into the intense smell of fresh, wet wood. The house is in its earliest stages of construction; only its frame has been erected. I can see nothing of the outside world but diffuse, eerie lights through the wet plastic.

    Clumps of wet sawdust stick to our feet. We sit on beams that will eventually form the ground floor of the house. From his pocket, James extracts rolling papers and an orange RX bottle with no label. He pinches some weed between his fingers, closes and pockets the bottle, and begins meticulously rolling a large joint in the darkness.

    This is mad good weed, he assures me. You'll see.

    Cool.

    The acoustics lull me; inside the plastic-draped house, the rain sounds like a purring goddess. I feel calm and good. The lonely glamour of being here, with him in the darkness and rain, makes me feel like we're confidantes.

    I say, I saw some cool shit two weekends ago.

    Yeah? He licks the edge of the paper.

    Yeah.

    Like?

    Nicole Larson getting it on with Lucy Sears. I can see in Nicole's bedroom from our upstairs bathroom window.

    I fucked Nicole once. Didn't know she went both ways.

    Yeah, usually her blinds are pulled. I've also seen Mr. Larson pissing in his garden sometimes at night.

    James chuckles. It keeps the rabbits and groundhogs out. It scares them. The scent of piss. Or maybe he's just marking his territory. Okay, here—you start it off.

    He passes me the neat joint, watches me.

    Um, you got a lighter?

FIRES

In silence, he fishes an orange Bic lighter from his pocket and presses it deliberately into my palm. I light up the joint, let the end smolder so it catches, and inhale. It isn't good weed—even I can tell that. Later I'll learn that people who are cool always claim their weed is superlative even when they know it's not. For the moment, though, I'm disappointed. But it'll still get us a little high, so I guess I don't mind. I drag a couple times, cough, and pass it back.

You applying to schools yet? I croak, after a halting mental treasure hunt for something relevant to say.

Hold it in, man.

What schools you applying to?

Shit. Duke, Yale, U-Penn. Some others. USC, Tulane.

Cool.

He passes it back to me when it's halfway gone, then stands and reaches above his head to grab a wooden beam, hauling himself into the air to do a series of spontaneous, snarling chin-ups. I see the lean, knotty muscles of his arms. Rain drums the plastic sheeting.

His feet thud in the sawdust and he takes the joint back, sits.

You're gonna get a football scholarship, right?

Mursey's helping me out.

It's not so unusual for a teacher or coach to become associated with a certain student, usually a precocious or excellent one, in whom he sees echoes of himself. He starts helping the student out, giving advice and writing recommendations, and becomes a mentor. That's how it is with James and Coach Mursey.

Maybe you'll go pro? I suggest.

Fuck, no, I'm nowhere near good enough. You gotta be fucking huge. I can get an athletic scholarship to a good school, that's about it, then I'm gonna study architecture.

Not play football?

Sure, I'll keep playing for a while. The game is fun, you know?

Besides, it'd probably break Coach's heart if I quit after next year.

Can I get one last one?

He hands me the joint, leaking smoke from his nostrils like a dragon. I finish it off, then kill it in the sawdust.

That *was* some good weed, I lie.

Yeah, no gravelly junk in there.

The wind finds a breach in the plastic sheeting and makes it whistle madly. The plastic is flapping in a churlish fury against the wooden beams, like a child throwing a tantrum. I notice James watching me. Shadows tend to soften faces, but they do the opposite to his. He has a baby's mouth, but he also has cheekbones like flint knives.

Why are you so fucking nervous? he asks.

I'm not nervous.

You look nervous.

Well, I'm not.

So you're cool?

Yeah, of course.

Sawdust gets in my nose and I sneeze, embarrassingly, causing minor vibrations of pleasure to ripple through my flesh. Being stoned makes the rain louder. Being stoned feels good. I want to stay like this all night.

Why don't we get higher, he says.

Smoke another one?

Nah, I got something else.

He digs into his pocket again and brings out a pile of junk—wadded paper, the RX bottle, rolling papers, a folded glossy pamphlet, and a rectangular tea tin. He opens the tin and takes out a reddish dime bag filled with powder instead of weed.

What's that?

You never done blow before?

FIRES

What, I guess, no.
But you're cool, right?
I—I guess, yeah. I mean, I don't know. What's it do, exactly?
A lightning flash momentarily illuminates us, its brightness transmuted by the water-streaked plastic into pale, dream-soft twilight. Darkness returns and I can't see a thing. Thunder gambols in the clouds.

It makes you feel terrific. But if you don't want to, it's cool. Personally I like to just try all fucking kinds of shit, take a thing as far as it'll go. But if you feel, you know, scared—I understand.
No, no. I want to do it.
Don't if you're scared. It's cool.
No, I do.
Okay, he says, then I'll cut it. He sets the tin beside him on the wooden beam, then takes a Swiss Army knife from his other pocket. He flips open the blade and presses the side of it down on the bag to crush up little rocks. As he breaks them up, he explains:

There's about a gram here. Maybe less. It's kind of yellowy, but I've tried it—it's tasty. You can tell how good this shit is by how quick it numbs your tongue. I'll cut like four real big lines for each of us. We could make it last longer, but for tonight it's better to just get high in one big burst. Plus I crushed up a Xanax and put it in there. You'll get real high. It's not like weed, it only lasts ten or fifteen minutes—and that's without the Xanax—and then you get jittery and come down unless you do more. Once you're coming down, though, you can get kinda strange.

Later, I will learn that casual drug users—especially in the first flush of their experience with a new drug—love to initiate non-users, detailing with hushed concentration the minutiae of a drug's use and effects, as if in order to get high one must adhere to an talismanic and jealously guarded set of procedures.

Okay, he says, we need something to do this off.

As he unfolds the glossy pamphlet he took from his pocket earlier, I ask, Where'd you get it?

Baltimore. Okay, look, we'll do it off this brochure. You got a dollar? Roll it up.

As I follow those directions, he opens the bag and deposits its contents on the glossy pamphlet, which is from Yale and depicts students grinning as gothic architecture glowers behind them. With the blade of his knife, James proceeds to carefully divide the nickel-sized heap of white powder into eight close lines which are significantly smaller than what I've seen in the movies. He gives me the bag to lick clean, and a moment later I cannot feel my tongue.

He does his four lines, then I do mine. It is a guilty thing to do. The dull clamor of the rain reverberates. As my sinuses burn, then go numb, I watch James lick invisible crumbs of dust from the brochure. He dips his fingers in a nearby puddle (rainwater has pooled inside the frame of the unfinished house), holds them to his nose, and inhales. His eyes gleam. I don't feel anything except a bit stoned.

What is this? I am thinking. What the hell? What the hell, what is this, I don't feel anything, I'm supposed to feel high but actually I feel normal, completely cogent, and my eyesight is crystal clear. My thoughts are—

Man, I say, one thing I really notice about people is their hands, if they have nice hands, if their hands have a nice shape. Some people have like stubby, doughy hands, or dry hands, but I always notice if somebody has beautiful hands. Amanda has good hands, that's one example.

She does, he says. She does have good hands, she has very sexy hands, her hands are sexy, at least if hands can be sexy, which they can, I guess that's what you're saying: they can. Me and the backup quarterback from Middletown had a threeway with her. Sometimes

FIRES

I think that picture of a train on Middletown's uniform looks like a rocket, did you ever notice that, the way they draw rocket ships in picture books, like you used to read when you were a kid.

    You've got good hands, I say. It's not that your hands are sexy, I'm not thinking anything sexual about your hands, just that they're good hands, so it's hard not to look at them. Man, my heart is really going. Thanks, man, I really, can I owe you or something—

    No, no, it's cool—

    No, man, I don't want to be a—

    It's okay, it's okay—

    Cool, I didn't mean anything by the thing about your hands, when I said about looking at your hands, okay. I'm just really high, I just feel like I want to just, just do something—

    Like you want to—

    Like I want to just—

    —just get up and go fucking—

    —yes, exactly—

    —like go hunting. You and me, to go hunting, if we went hunting, wouldn't that be funny, Danfield, if we went hunting, what would we hunt? Ha, ha.

    Deer and humans, certain brands of cars, people who like Dave Matthews—

    —Dave Matthews himself—

    We have no guns.

    My dad was a fucking Marine—

    —so he has them, your dad has them, has guns?

    Yeah, a couple .22s, a .38, a couple rifles, locked up but I can get them, I like them, I know how to use them, it's like they're a special kind of hand if you know how to use them. You don't have to remember how to use your hand. You just use it. You don't think, you just use it. Like anything, I just have to keep, you know, moving, like one of those sharks, keep moving, and that is the thing that sets me apart, that thing, the never stop moving, that's what that is. This thing that makes other people want me—do you know that people want me—not even women but guys too, and I mean I'll be honest it's flattering, I'm not trying to brag but it's flattering—

You really—don't take this the wrong way, I wouldn't say it except I feel like I know exactly what you're talking about and it's strange, but I actually have wondered what it's like to have that ability—

No, that's not even the thing, though, it's like just a side effect of like being not able to stop moving, you know I have to push myself all the time, I have to—

Fuck, my head hurts, is it supposed to?

Sometimes it does.

Like in the front side of the temple?

Yeah, sure. Maybe.

Jesus.

You're fine. Don't worry.

I know, I'm just—shit. That was weird. That was fast. That was so *fast*.

Yeah. You're still high, just not as high.

I know. I know. I know.

It's all right. Calm down. That was just the big rush. Calm down.

I am. Hey, by the way like, I didn't mean anything—I don't know what I was talking about, that was weird. Cool?

Don't worry about it.

No, I just mean—I didn't mean anything weird, it was just some weird stuff I said off the top of my head, it was, like, totally pointless.

Our conversation stops. Rain batters the plastic sheeting. My chest feels like a hollow tree in which a sparrow is trapped, fluttering in hysterics. My breath comes in short gasps and my throat is bitter and dry. James is composed, though. An explosion of thunder makes me flinch.

FIRES

Fuck, I'm still so *high*, I stammer.

He only grins in the darkness, and his grin makes me nervous. My hands are shaking; I don't know it yet, but I am already beginning to crash. I am ashamed about the stuff I said. My nose drips. I feel a creeping sense of misery and embarrassment. Skin breaks as I gnaw my lip.

James leans forward and rests on his elbows, watching me intensely. He exudes physical strength in his movements.

Calm down, he says. You're just starting to come down, that's all. This is early. Must be the Xanax, or maybe just cheap coke.

I'm calm, I insist. I am calm. I am calm.

The smell of rain and wet sawdust is suddenly overpowering, exhausting. I *am* calm, I repeat above the dramatic thudding in my chest. In the black shadows, the angles of his face begin to look skeletal, less cherubic, a little eerie. Warm rain pounds harder than ever outside. The wet darkness seems to muffle all speech.

Disoriented emotions swim after each other in my blood, taint my thoughts. I shiver, but the air isn't cold. My mind feels sandblasted. I long, suddenly, to go home and masturbate. But I am not capable of that; my legs are too numb and James is too magnetic. That's okay, though. It's fine just to sit here.

The rain batters away at the plastic. James keeps pensively knotting his fingers, as if making a cage, or a trap. I don't feel like getting up. Neither does he, I guess, because we don't move until late in the night, waiting out the rain, floating in the emotional backwash of the drugs. At some point I say, perhaps with a vaguely pleading tone, Let's do this again, okay? It's been a while since we even, you know, talked and shit. And he nods, flashing his insatiable grin.

I catch a cold during the night and I'm sick for the next week or so, sequestered in my room with hot soup and novels, and in the months that follow I hardly see James, never mind talk to him. But it isn't as though I'm preoccupied by the possibility. I get involved with a girl from my English class, concentrating much effort on the eradication of our mutual virginity.

I don't see him much during his senior year, either. The football team, expected to be champions for a third consecutive year, falters inexplicably at the end of their season and limps into the playoffs, where they get demolished. James has already been accepted to Yale, though.

But his reckless personality seems tempered by the time graduation rolls around, and he withdraws from social circles. Every year there are a few scrupulously insouciant students who are too hip to attend graduation, but James's absence is a minor shock, considering that he's valedictorian. In summer, I see him around once in a while, and in the fall he goes off to college and I start 12th grade.

When I enter Yale a year later, after giving a valedictory speech of my own, James is taking the year off, so I haven't seen him in two years by the time he returns. Though still popular, he is different. A new, hard persona has solidified. His face sometimes, particularly when he's alone or unselfconscious, looks like igneous rock; it is merciless and secretly isolated.

* * *

But forget about James for now. He isn't the only thing that's on my mind after we pass each other that hot day when I am walking across campus to meet Ruth at the coffee shop. I am also thinking about the sticky heat, and Ruth, and the sticky sex we are going to have tonight, and how I'm almost out of cigarettes.

Killing Time

Ruth has decided to come with me to Atlantic City. We've got tickets for the Greyhound to New Jersey on Saturday. The week before spring break we spend lying around with lights off, talking in whispers, smoking, drinking, listening to music, having less sex than usual since she's on her period.

Friday night, we go to Zack's apartment. Not many people are there, and it is a quiet, edgy scene through which Jeffrey Dahmer wanders, pushing his big white-brown head into laps. Zack and Nick have bought coke and people are doing it in the bedroom with clipped plastic straws. Ruth and I sit on the sofa. She's drunk.

Reece Robinson and a guy with the shaved head emerge from Zack's bedroom with wet noses and flickering eyes. Reece is smoking a ragged cigar that burns unevenly. Zack, beside us on the sofa, finishes a Rolling Rock and opens another one.

I'm going to Japan over break, he says for no particular reason, and no one answers. The Japanese are insane, I swear, he adds. Zack's an odd person. We're not what I would call friends—more like acquaintances. I used to come to this apartment a lot last year to buy drugs.

Reece approaches and sits with us, puffing his cigar. Smoke twines in the air. The White Stripes play "Sugar Never Tasted So Good."

What's that smell, man? That bitter smell?

I packed like ten lines in this cigar.

Zack offers me a cigarette, but he's smoking French things that smell like gerbils and I wave it away.

More people emerge from the bedroom. Ruth is being quiet. Jeffrey Dahmer nestles his head in her lap and she strokes his ears. He's a friendly, sad dog, and it's unfortunate that he has to live here. Ruth leans toward me, so close her lips are touching my ear.

Let's go.
Don't you want to finish your drink?
Let's go.

As we walk back to her room, she leans against me.
Are you okay?
Just tired.
Why?
Don't know.
    I wrap an arm around her small shoulders, but I feel strange, too. She has sobered up somewhat. The night is warm and clear, and above us elm trees shake heavy batches of fresh leaves.
    We pass the cemetery, which is locked and dark. A stray cat, skin draped on birdlike bones, skulks down the street. A child's doll has been hanged from a tree.
    Later, we lie quietly, uneasily, among the rumpled sheets of her bed. The lights are off. Flat, faraway music and warm breeze come through the window. We don't tease each other or kiss.
    I hope you like the beach, I murmur.
    I will.
    I hope so.
    I'm lying on my back, wearing boxers which are limp from being washed a million times. Ruth is on her stomach, arms curled under her breasts, face pushed into a pillow. She's wearing a t-shirt and panties.
    Darkness huddles somberly around us and we listen to ghostly, distant noises of the world outside: a song being played hollowly at a party below . . . voices drifting up from the quad, flat and inaudible. The world seems huge, dark, and full of heavy, sad possibilities.
    I say, What if we ever had a kid?
    That will never happen.

FIRES

(My heart tightens.) Why not?
Because I don't ever want a child.
Oh.
Why, what did you think?
Nothing.
I'd be a bad mother.
No, you wouldn't.
Don't be stupid.

 I grow silent, wanting a cigarette but not wanting to rise. The tree outside her window rustles with soft breeze and thoughts move through my mind slowly, like leaves on the surface of a lake. My tongue is raw and inflamed. Too many cigarettes.
 I hope you like the beach, I murmur.

The Beach

We get into Atlantic City around noon.
 The sun is like fire. I squint behind sunglasses and my hair drips with sweat. Ruth is wearing a tank top and her shoulders glisten with lotion. We catch the jitney, which takes us almost to my grandmother's doorstep, and when we climb the porch steps, the door swings open to greet us, releasing a blast of frigid air. My grandmother—a bear-like, effusive woman—fawns over Ruth.
 My grandmother has a full-time aide (his title is something like *caregiver* or *home assistant*, but she just calls him "my nurse") who my parents hired after her hip surgery and who is supposed to take care of her, help her around, do housework. He has prepared a big lunch and it is obvious my grandmother runs him ragged.
 We eat at her dining room table, sandwiches and crabmeat salad with cold pasta, and when my grandmother spills her V-8 juice, the

ANTOSCA

nurse dutifully starts scrubbing it out of the white tablecloth. I notice his glance at Ruth, whose body is glistening with chilled sweat, and who has assumed a convincingly innocent quality.

My grandmother keeps asking Ruth what she studies and how many siblings she has (no, she says—I glance at her but she does not look at me) and where she's from (Vermont) and is it cold there and would she like some green grapes? Because they don't have the seeds, dear. Eat more salad than that, dear—you'll starve! My granddaughters are just like you. They don't eat *anything* . . .

And Ruth is laughing and smiling and totally charming my grandmother.

After we finish the meal (and the tablecloth is whisked off to the laundry room) my grandmother orders us down to the beach, shooing us from the table. He'll take care of it! she says grandly.

So we go upstairs, put our duffel bags in our bedrooms (in theory, we're sleeping in separate rooms) and change into bathing suits. Then we take towels out of the hallway closet, rub sweet-smelling lotion on each other and walk down to the beach.

The weather stays hot and bright and clear as glass. After that first glorious afternoon by the water, we are as dark as Trojan soldiers and our feet are in pain from the shells and hot sand. When we lick each other, we taste salt water.

I was afraid that the unease that plagued me in preceding days would linger during spring break—but no. The feeling melts away. There is only the sun on our faces.

My grandmother loves Ruth. They sit at the living room table one evening and Ruth helps her clip coupons. My grandmother keeps asking if Ruth is Greek (like our family) and when Ruth says she isn't sure, she doesn't think so, my grandmother keeps exclaiming how much Ruth looks like an old schoolmate from her girlhood in Kephissia. Later, Ruth vanishes into the kitchen and gets a bowl of grapes from the fridge; she and my grandmother eat them together at the table.

    The days pass. Seashells dig into our feet and waves knock us down. Our tans molt. We feel fantastic. Life smells like suntan lotion and liquor—which we've smuggled down in our duffel bags—and the ocean. At lunch we eat subs with Italian deli meat and there are potato salad and orange juice and subtle glances from the nurse. Then we walk down to the beach. Afterward, exhausted by the ocean, we chill ourselves in the air conditioning.
    At dinnertime we walk a few blocks in our sandals and eat pizza and meatball subs. At night, with the lifeguards gone, we go down to the water and sit on the empty beach, drinking whiskey and watching dark waves roar. The ocean is candy-black at night. The stars are like dagger points, and in the flat distance we see the lights of yachts and buoys.

    In the evenings, my parents call. How are things? my dad asks. Do you want to talk to your mother?
    And my mother will say, Are you wearing enough sunscreen?
    And, When are we going to meet this girl?

    We curl up on the living room rug late at night, eating ice cream. My grandmother apparently asked the nurse to go shopping before we got there and buy "things kids like." So the freezer is full of ice cream and frozen hot dogs.
    The TV is on, but quietly. Ruth has stretched out on her stomach and keeps playing with the remote. She's giggly and a little hyper— she gets like this after eating sugary things. I roll on top of her, biting

her shoulders.

Quit, you asshole. You'll wake up your grandma.

Fuck it.

I want to take you home to Maryland, I whisper. I want you to come home to my neighborhood and meet my parents. I want to kiss every part of—

To shut me up, she kisses me. I bite her ear and she claws my neck, then elbows me in the chest when I try to get her shirt up.

Agh—fuck, you knocked the wind out of me.

Good, you jerk.

We sprawl out on the carpet to finish our melting ice cream. The news is on. A senator tells reporters his private life is private, then the weather report begins. A heat wave is sweeping the United States and there is a drought all up the East Coast. Two major forest fires rage—one in Colorado and another in New Mexico. Ice cream trickles down Ruth's spoon onto her finger. I lick it off and kiss her cold sweet mouth.

It's got to end, of course. School is starting again—there will be another week of classes, then finals. And by mid-May we'll be free. We haven't decided yet what we're doing over the summer. We'll each have to go home first, but we're talking about subletting an apartment in New York or Boston for June, July, August.

The night before we leave, we sit on the porch together, sharing a deck chair. Through the picture window we can see Grandma and her nurse watching *Dick van Dyke*. We smell the ocean. Around us the city is full of little noises, voices from blocks over, radios, sirens. My grandmother's street is quiet; only old women and Welsh corgis live here.

Some of the incandescent bliss of the previous days is dissolving, slipping away. Slowly but inescapably, the real world is coming back.

FIRES

It brings with it a tinge of unease. I can't put my finger, exactly, on what's wrong. It's just that something unpleasant inside my chest won't go to sleep. So I say—

I love you.

It's the first time I've actually said it since the first time I said it. I haven't needed to. For a moment she says nothing.

We are stretched out together, pressed to each other in the deck chair. There isn't much room, so she's partly in my lap. I am kissing her neck. Slowly she whispers: Do you mean that?

Of course.

Really?

Really.

You know I love you, Jon. I love you. I love you. I do love you.

On the next street, a child laughs. The laughter is soft, musical. Words play back in my mind like taunts. *Do you mean that?* I think I did. But I also thought speaking it would make me feel better. It hasn't.

We lie a while longer in the dark. I listen to my own slow, easy breathing. Her bare shoulders are a warm satiny brown in the darkness. Idly, unthinking, I glance at the picture window.

My grandmother's nurse is watching us. His head is turned away from the TV and he's staring out the picture window, watching. Watching Ruth. As if he has been for a long time. Noticing I've seen him, he calmly turns back to the TV. I feel a hot stripe of anger. Unexpected, heating my chest.

I stare through the glass, silently daring him to turn his head, to look at her again. I *want* him to look, I realize—because if he does, the jealousy that's clicking its teeth in my ear will be drawn out and made to fight. I want him to look because if he does, he's going to become a lot of different people. He'll be every person who Ruth fucked before me, every one of those lantern-jawed, no-faced bodies who've been submerged in my brain as I soaked in the sun, as I baked on the sand. Except he doesn't look.

And all of those figures, jostled loose by a casually lascivious glance, begin to bump against each other in my thoughts like drowned corpses rising to the surface. Ruth—whose warm, walnut-dark head is pressed against my arm—notices nothing.

Morning, and we go to the bus station. It is early, but the sun's out. Now it irritates us; we are bleary-eyed and haven't slept and don't want blazing light in our eyes. We fucked most of the night, in bursts of violent, barely muffled sex that neither of us expected or understood. Seagulls wheel. People have faces of plaster and dust. A seeing eye dog has a child's tasseled baton in its mouth. We buy tickets. We wait on long wooden benches until the Greyhound arrives. Then we find seats and stow our luggage overhead and ignore everyone. Once we are moving, Ruth sleeps, muttering in her dreams.

We pass dried-out landscapes on the way back. Tinderbox landscapes. Things have wilted in the heat and it isn't even May.

Drifting

BACK AT SCHOOL WE'RE EXHAUSTED. Our skin is dry and brown and there's no respite from the heat. The dorms aren't air conditioned, of course. We live in Ruth's room—our room, essentially—but things aren't quite the same.

The last week of classes goes by. Still no rain. Less than seven days are left until I have to go home. I watch TV in the common room while Ruth is at work. One of the girls who lives on Ruth's floor—Lauren, the redhead—is addicted to CNN, and we watch

FIRES

dull specials on Israel and drilling in the Arctic Wildlife Preserve. Most of the news concerns the heat wave. Unexpected wildfires on the East Coast—the *East* Coast—have gotten out of control. One has eaten several homes in West Virginia.

Anxiety and jealousy make it hard for me to concentrate on anything. Most nights, Ruth and I have brutal sex, and, once, she starts crying what seem like tears of rage, shaking with violent, angry sobs.

And late at night, when she is sleeping, I often drift out to the empty common room with a bottle of whiskey to watch TV—news of heat waves, news of fire—and listen to the warm dry night murmuring outside the window. Sometimes on these nights I find myself afraid.

violence

I buzz up to Zack's in the listless afternoon.

The door clicks and I enter a dim vestibule where the walls are streaked with grime. The gray staircase is speckled with cigarette butts. I walk up to the second floor. On the landing, empty liquor bottles sit like sick birds.

Zack, when he opens the door, is pale and nervous.

Good to see *you*, man, he says. He is shirtless. Haven't seen you in a, a while. There wasn't anybody outside, was there?

I don't think so.

Come in, come in.

We go up another flight of steps to the loft area. A smell of stale weed. Wrinkled twenties and fifties are piled on a desk, and a grimy computer displays windows of downloaded porn.

Zack is the only one home. His hands are trembling and he's blinking a lot. He apologizes, profusely, for having no beer.

We haven't had any food for like a, a week. I owe some money, just a little, but it's better for me not to, to go outside.

The store's a half-block away, man.

I've been. I've been eating dog food.

I see. Hey, where *is* the dog?

I, I don't know. I haven't seen him for a while.

Oh. Jesus. Uh, well, how was Japan?

Japan?

Sighing, I take a seat on the leather sofa. His bewilderment is sad. The place is a wreck. He has apparently been organizing CDs; they're scattered around in half-assed heaps. Zack gestures at them with a groan of despair.

This is what happens, he says with anguish. *This* is what happens when you do too much drugs. Your music gets all mixed up. You put CDs back in the wrong cases.

He pauses, grabbing his chin, like a general surveying the infantry arrayed against him.

Some cases are *empty*, he shouts. Where are the CDs? He rubs his eyes. They're in *other* cases. Frogs in the Mudhoney case. Mudhoney in Dr. Octagon. The endless cycle. And they're all, they're all scratched. *Mermaid Avenue* won't even play. Where does it end? I have to face facts: *Some. Are. Missing.*

Just download the music and burn it, man.

Some of my CDs. Are *missing*.

There's genuine horror in his voice. In a low, raw whisper, he says—I'll tell you what's awful. Bands that don't put the name of the album on the actual, physical CD. It's the fucking bane of my existence. It's my. My *bête noire*.

Zack.

Hm?

Calm down a minute. I want to ask you something.

Ask, ask. I'm calm.

Remember before break? We were talking one time? And you said you heard things about Ruth, like from before. What did you mean, exactly—what things? Specifically, I mean.

Oh, man, come on. So what if she, like, did stuff? You've, you've got your head all in the wrong place, Jon.

So she fucked a lot of guys? Before me, I mean?

Come on, man. She's cool.

I spit out an exasperated, almost involuntary snarl—he raises his arms defensively.

Don't get mad at *me*, man. Hell, don't get mad at her, either. She's a cool girl. I love Ruth. I don't think she'd cheat on you.

I try to control my anger. I push it down because I am very good at pushing things down. Zack looks at me, wary.

You're not mad, are you?

No. After a pause, I say—Who?

Who?

Who were they? That she was with.

I dunno. What does it matter, anyway? Why do you even want to know? I mean, I think she hooked up with that guy Austin once. Maybe others. But what good's it gonna do to find out names? (He is looking at me warily, keeping his distance.) It'll just make things worse. You'll see them around. You know, get pissed off. Better not to know.

Right before me, who was she with? That's what I want to know.

Oh, I don't know, man. Most of what I heard was from, like, last year.

But earlier this year. This winter. Come on.

Far as I know she wasn't with anybody.

She was.

Well then she must of kept it a secret.

There is another sighing pause, and he keeps glancing at me as if to make sure I'm not going to start breaking things.

You know, there's really, like, no reason to be angry at the guys she hooked up with, man. If you are, I mean. Angry. Or—did something happen? Did she say anything?

No.

Well, there you go, dude. That's what I'm saying. I—

Wait. Wait a second.

What?

Did *you* ever sleep with her?

He hesitates. His hand twitches. He says: Um.

You *did*.

He looks away. Yeah. Okay. Once.

I contain explosive anger. Were you going to tell me?

Well, I, I wasn't sure, you know? But, uh, I'm glad you asked. Because, you know, I wouldn't, um, lie to you.

Great.

You pissed off?

No, no. Wait, it was before I was with her, right?

Yeah, of course, man! So, like, listen. Want to smoke up and help me sort my collection?

Sorry. I gotta go.

He shrugs, relieved. Then he discovers his bong, knocks over a stack of *Hustlers*, and starts packing the bowl as I get up to leave. Pull the outer door hard, he says. Sometimes it doesn't close.

He takes a bong rip and watches me go down to the door. I walk down the filthy stairs, not bothering to pull the outer door hard as I go out to the street, into the beastly sun.

After dark, my mother calls.

Do you know your grades yet? she asks.

FIRES

Bs in everything.

Hm! And how's Ruth?

Good. How's home?

Your dad finished teaching last week, and we saw Aunt Jean and your cousins on Saturday. It's hot here. Have you been watching the news?

Yeah.

The fires—you know?

They're near us.

Mm-hm. You'll see when you get home. You can see smoke over the mountain. There are sirens every day.

That near?

Oh, yeah.

Aren't you worried?

No, dear.

But they're *that* close? Really?

Don't sound so anxious. They'll get it under control.

Um, okay, then. Anything else?

Looking forward to having you home. Got your ticket?

Yeah. Saturday.

Talking with her leaves me tense. She means well, but her optimism is like sugar crunching between my teeth. My mother's the kind of person who believes, deep down, that bad things just don't happen to good people.

After her phone call I watch CNN in the common room. The fires are all over Maryland, Virginia, and West Virginia. Like monsters on old sea charts. I get unexpected butterflies in my stomach. CNN shows footage of fires raging in South Carolina, in Georgia, rural fires that have burned for days, threatening to encroach on suburbs.

I rise and walk downstairs, go outside in the red haze of a sunset.

ANTOSCA

I envision fire destroying my high school: benign, benevolent old Bondurant High—the paint peeling off the walls, trophies melting in their cases, class photographs bubbling, sweating, blackening—and I feel clammy.

The sun hits the horizon and bursts like an egg yolk. Red light smears the sky, and I wonder if the fires are sending ash into the atmosphere, staining it red.

I think about the fires. Plastic siding melting off my house. The TV antenna wilting into hot black tar. But no . . . the fire will be out in a couple days, normalcy restored—so other kids can remember the place like I do. I am just seeing the nightmare scenario.

The vivid sun drowns and disappears. Slowly it sucks down the red effluvia it smeared on the horizon, leaving the sky a bloodless gray-blue.

In the gathering dusk I begin to walk. The twilight is a husky color when I reach the New Haven green, the large park with winding paths and old elms a few blocks from central campus. I find a bench and sit in the gloom.

The day is gone but I can still feel the heat. I do not think about Ruth yet. Not directly. I gnaw my thumbnail. Again the images return—flames eating our house, our neighborhood, the parks and soccer fields, the Christmas tree farms, the sagging farmhouses that still exist on patches of land between developments and access roads. A weird shudder passes through me. I spit a bit of my thumbnail on the bench.

Lighting a cigarette, I allow myself at last to think of Ruth. There's anger in my chest. I exhale smoke, ghostly gray. Nothing justifies this—this hot, snarling thing in my heart.

I stare at the trees and into the warm, blue-black darkness. I drag on my cigarette, then look at it, an angry jewel in the listless dark. For a long time I can't look away. And when I do, there's a scarlet fingerprint burned on my vision.

FIRES

We are on the edge of a fight. I've forced her into it, aware in some masochistic fold of my brain that I want this. And I can't stop myself from wanting it.

I've come to Ruth's room and been so sullen and uncommunicative that she's a picture of silent confusion. I feel guilty and immature, but my inability to control my anger is both impossible to transcend and genuinely unsettling. This isn't me.

Ruth sits on her bed, arms curled around her knees, and watches me pace. She says bitterly—

Why are you doing this?

I'm not doing anything.

Yes, you are. You're furious.

I look at her. We are both a little buzzed—she was reading a book and sipping apple juice and whiskey when I walked in, and I had shots from her liquor shelf when I got here.

Ask me why.

Stop it, Jon.

Ask me.

Okay, then. Why.

Her face is obstinate but her chin keeps crumpling. She's still brown from the beach.

I want to know about—ah, fuck—okay, how many guys have you been with?

What?

You heard me.

Uh, *none* since you. I've been faithful to you.

You *know* what I mean. *Before* me.

What *difference* does it make? Why the fuck are you doing this?

She throws up her palms in frustration, her voice high and unsteady. My anger is a swollen presence in me, something ripe that wants harvesting. It's a visceral feeling, like an organ pumping beside my liver and lungs.

What *difference* it makes is that, that—that you're being *stupid*. You sleep around and you end up with dangerous guys and it's just—what's *wrong* with you? Why would you be like that? You end up with some guy who strangles you and then you won't tell me who hurt you, and, and, whose fault is it—

You have no fucking idea what you're talking about.

Don't tell me that! I—what I know is that you've fucked how many guys? You won't tell me. True or false, more than twenty.

Jon . . .

Fuck you.

Her hair is in tangles and there are tears behind her eyes, but the violence of my insult makes something lock down. She retreats; her face goes stony. She reacts like I imagine most intelligent women would if their lover hit them—sympathies shutting down, mind moving from avenues of reconciliation to avenues of escape.

No, wait. I'll be alone. Sudden vertigo, the ground dropping out. A stab of terror, a rush of guilt. She's going to leave. Confused thoughts lock horns in my head. I want to be with her, but more than that I simply *don't want to be alone.* Maybe it's not too late. I stammer—

I guess maybe we—we should do something new.

Like what? Her face is swollen, red beneath the tan, as if she *has* been slapped.

Something new—for us. For our, you know, for us.

(I don't even know what I mean. I've got a vague idea of a trip— we'll drive somewhere, be drunk and in love, like in Atlantic City. But I'm angry and stubborn and don't want to give ground by suggesting it myself.)

You mean. You mean you want to, like, get with other people?

Helpless, I shrug. The moment is gone too fast to snatch it back. Ruth just sits miserably on the bed. Tears exist somewhere in her

FIRES

dark brown eyes but she contains them, although she is lugubriously biting her lower lip. Everything is nightmarishly slow and she doesn't know what to do with her hands. They tremble.

She tells me, Please just go.

There's a moment where I'm lingering there, trying to decide if I can salvage something, but it all seems to slip through my fingers and I feel beaten, banished.

I go into the hall and the redhead is there, her arms crossed and her eyes accusatory. I hurry downstairs and the shadows seem hot. I want to pull out my tongue with pliers. Outside in the dark I slouch on a bench and smoke a cigarette, but it loosens vomit in my gut and I have to hold myself very still so I won't throw up. My drunkenness isn't from alcohol but self-disgust. Later I get up and walk around in the dark for a while.

My hallway is deserted. Behind someone's door I hear low groaning porn. We've got less than forty-eight hours—then Ruth will go to Vermont and I'll be on a train to Maryland. I drink some whiskey, feeling loathsome. I drift into the dark, empty common room and turn on the TV. A *Biography* of the Marquis de Sade is on. Later, the History Channel has a special about something called the Big Blowup, a forest fire that killed eighty-seven people and destroyed three million acres at the turn of the century.

I switch to CNN. International news about an assassination in the Middle East, then more weather. The endless, insufferable heat. Pictures of the fires. I flip to the Weather Channel, and there's an hour-long special on. *Wildfire: Natural Wonder . . . from Hell.* I watch with a special kind of terror.

I flip back to CNN, which is showing footage of a crisis center thrown together at an elementary school. I'm not giving it my full attention. I'm wondering whether the siding on my house would burn or melt. A newscaster with a mike is standing in a cafeteria and people are milling behind her.

Holy shit, I yell. *Miller!* (I had him for high school calculus. I'd never mistake that face.) Holy shit, I say.

That crisis center was in *Bondurant*.

But the segment is already over. Digging my cell phone out of my pocket, I call home. There's staticky ringing that goes on and on. The answering machine picks up and my own voice speaks across years (*You've reached the Danfields'! . . .*), a younger version of me. I sound healthy.

I call again. The hairy, staticky ringing drags on. Finally I hang up.

Getting up, I pace the dark room. A warm breeze comes in the window. The taste of blood spreads across my tongue; I am sinking my teeth into the inside of my lip.

I go to the window and spit. My watch says one AM. But I know she'll be sitting awake.

The phone, like a distress signal, rings five or six times before she picks up. I say mournfully—

Ruth, I'm sorry.

Are you.

Really. I'm sorry. I'm drunk. I know it doesn't change anything, but there's no way I'm going to sleep if I didn't talk to you. So. I'm sorry.

Great. Sleep well.

I mean, I don't know why I—went off like that. And I feel like shit. Don't know what else to say right now. So, yeah.

Silence.

Sorry. I'll, uh, talk to you tomorrow?

If you want.

Goodnight.

Yeah.

FIRES

She hangs up before I do. I sit in the dark and taste blood.

* * *

I dream I'm back in Bondurant, the sky filled by lovely purple clouds. I wander, reaching a playground where kids play on the slides, and I can *see* giggles float out of them like soap bubbles. Later I walk across a neighbor's lawn, fresh-cut grass sticking to the soles of my feet, and spot a happy dog.

* * *

What wakes me isn't the TV or morning traffic, but my cell phone vibrating, and, bleary, I sit up and fumble for it.
Hello?
Morning, dear.
Hi, Mom. (Rubbing my eyes.)
Saw you on the Caller ID.
It was like one AM. Where were you?
Oh, we went to a dinner party at the Bookers' and stayed late.
Well, I was—
We tried to call you earlier in the evening, but you didn't answer.
Yeah. My phone was off. Sorry about that.
You have to change your Amtrak ticket. We're leaving for a few days because of the fires.
You're being evacuated.
Well, yeah. It's not like houses are on fire or anything. But the air is bad. So we're going to your grandmother's for the week. You'll need to change your ticket and meet us there.
Which grandma? Grandma at the beach?
Mm-hm. My mother.

ANTOSCA

Well, what about our house? Aren't you *worried*?
Oh no, they're going to put it out before it gets anywhere near us—
But—
—and besides, the real problem is air quality. That's why we're going. (That's a laugh; air quality in Atlantic City is abysmal.) You can see dirty smoke from the mountains—it looks awful.
Good god, Mom, how close *is* the fire?
Three or four miles, at least. It's in the mountains.
Jesus.
No, no, it's not as bad as it—
Mom, I saw on the news—I saw Mr. Miller from BHS. At, like, a crisis center or something. I mean, it looked like this thing is huge.
God, Jon, you sound almost panicked! Calm down—they're just setting up cots in the elementary school. We saw the CNN thing here, too, and from what I hear it was completely out of proportion—half those people they showed were just VFW volunteers who had nothing to do but stand around. In any case, I have to go—your father can't find his razor. Have a good train ride, honey—call us before you leave. And calm down, don't worry so much. See you at the beach.
She hangs up. So I'm going to the beach again. Without Ruth. But I don't want to, really. I want to go home.
Maybe Ruth could come to the beach with me, and things will be like before: a glorious, sun-soaked adventure. That fantasy lasts perhaps three seconds before I lie down, curling into a fetal position.

wandering, Bed

Ruth's voice is bleary and raw.
    I feel horrible, she says through the phone. Don't come over.
    Are you okay?
    Give me a couple hours.
    Ruth, I'm really sorry.
    I'm gonna lie down now.
    Okay. Feel better. I'll come by later.
    When she hangs up, I am alone. The elm tree rustles, a dry, insipid noise. Cars bleat . . . my head thuds. I want to go into a coma for a few hours.
    A bottle of rum sitting by the TV begs me to have a drink, which I do. Then I go downstairs into the heat, where wilted students sit on wilted grass, drinking beer and waiting for the semester to end. I start walking. Murderous heat. Squirrels crouch in the shade.
    I cross the green, where a woman is clutching a naked, sunburned baby on a bench. I go onto Temple Street. An electronic billboard at the intersection says the temperature is ninety-eight. I walk to the coffee shop.
    The air conditioning raises goose bumps. I slump in a booth and drink an iced espresso and want rum and Ruth. On the sidewalk, a woman slaps a child. I see James Dearborn across the street, eyes invisible beneath his baseball cap. He's bothering a homeless person or something, pointing his finger, accusing, as the homeless person tries to shuffle away. A bedraggled schnauzer, tongue dangling, lopes by.

    Leaving the shop in mid-afternoon, I go to the movies. I am almost alone in the theater. I try to be soothed by the darkness and air conditioning.
    The movie's in a Spanish-like language, possibly Spanish. I fall

asleep. When an usher wakes me, the credits are rolling.

Outside, the day is swollen; the light seems diluted and hazy. Humid heat smells of engine grease. The hour creeps toward five. Again I call Ruth.

Am I allowed over now?

Whatever. I don't care.

After the phone call, I stand on the sidewalk, sluggish, watching homeless people slump against buildings. Sweat drips down me.

The walk to Saybrook feels like I'm trudging through tar or bacon fat. A group of guys loiter outside her dorm, smoking Camels and talking about a science final. Sweat glistens on their shoulders. They are waiting for night, for the cooler air.

It is dark and humid in the dorm, where heat has gone stale. I trudge up four flights, breathing stagnant air, to her hallway. A girl I've never seen before slumps in the common room, drinking bottled water. She's wearing a sports bra and Lycra shorts.

I knock on Ruth's door.

There's a small thud of her feet hitting the floor as she rolls out of bed. They pad up to the door. It opens.

Come in.

A whiskey bottle is open on her desk; an old Styrofoam container is a cigarette graveyard. Ruth's eyes are red, and it reminds me of the night we met. Her mouth is sulking. A pair of my boxers hug her hips and she's wearing a limp t-shirt. When she tries to smile, the effort falters and resentment flares, then subsides, in her face.

I've been drinking all day, she says with bitterness. I feel like shit. Thanks a lot.

Not a healthy way to deal with an emotionally traumatic experience.

You're an emotionally traumatic experience, you fucking asshole.

I'll grant you that.

FIRES

A pause. No breeze is blowing. Ruth sighs irritably.

Come in. It's too hot to stand here.

I enter her room, which is dark but warm. With sorrowful slowness, she lies down on the bed and curls up.

Can I lie down with you?

Fine. But *don't touch*. It's too hot, and I'll throw up on you.

Okay.

I lie gingerly on the edge of the bed. It is hard not to touch her—the bed's so narrow. She turns away. We lie in the quiet shadows. Voices from four floors below, on the sidewalk, drift up.

In a flat voice, I tell her about the fires. I tell her I am not going home, but to Atlantic City. I don't invite her. It would be a hopeless, dumb, desperate thing to ask.

She turns so I can see her face. Her breath smells like liquor. Nothing moves. Nothing happens. I drowse. A dream unravels in which I smell fresh-cut grass and dogs bark at the sun.

When I wake, the room is full of dusk and shadows. Ruth's half-asleep and gazing sightlessly at me. It must be around eight. Voices come from downstairs. They're setting up a party below us, in the Sexplex. My skin feels sticky, chafed.

Ruth. You okay?

Yeah.

I'm gonna take a shower. You got a clean towel?

Mm. In the closet.

Quietly I get out of bed, get a towel, then walk down the hall to the bathroom. I turn cool water on, undress, and step into the shower. The water strips dry sweat from my body like a coat of old paint. I imagine it is morning, I'm just getting up. This hot, horrible day never happened. I rub exhaustion from my eyes.

When I go back to her room, music is drifting up from below. And many voices. She watches me dress, the anger gone from her

face. She is cool, passive.
 I murmur, Want to go to the party?
 Um. Later.
 Yeah?
 I want to lie here a while. She pauses, breathing shallowly. You go if you want, and I'll be down.
 I understand that she wants me to go alone. I slip shoes on, making sure I have my keys. Breathing quietly, I open the door to go.
 She says, Hey.
 Yeah?
 You'll sleep here tonight, won't you?
 Yeah. Of course.
 She nods softly in the darkness, and I slip out.

Girl's Bedroom

ON THE THIRD FLOOR, I can feel the building vibrating beneath me. The Sexplex is a party suite that takes up the first two floors. I descend to the second floor and a stench of bodies hits my lungs. A hundred sweaty people, at least, are jammed in the hallway. On huge speakers, an old Chili Peppers cover of Hendrix is playing.

Zack spots me through the crush and fights his way over. He's reeling drunk, his eyes bloodshot, his lips a funny blue color. I help him into a bedroom. The room belongs to a guy named Tim who owns a hamster called Pol Pot. People squat under a cloud of smoke; half-empty tequila bottles, juice boxes, and milk cartons litter the desk. Pol Pot cowers in her wire cage. I fill a plastic cup with tequila and milk and steal a salt shaker. Zack sits on the floor and I kneel beside him. I sip my drink—then pour salt on my tongue, shuddering.

Reece is here too, and so is a girl named Alison who I woke up

FIRES

next to once, long ago. Some guy whose nickname is Tea Bag is dry-heaving. It's too dark to see the others.

Zack is grabbing my arm. He wants to know why Ruth isn't with me. He wants to know if we're still together. We had an argument, I say. Things are kind of shaky.

You—you guys had a fight?

She had too much to drink. So did I.

She. She's drunk?

Alison, so skinny she might disappear, touches my leg. She has the bluish, horribly withered biceps of a genuinely anorexic girl. I gulp the potion in my cup. I blanch.

I gotta piss, Zack slurs. He stands, staggering over people's legs as they half-heartedly get out of his way. I am now pressed against Alison. I'm scared of her intentions. She pats my knee, comforting, for no reason, and I get the feeling she is about to pounce. Mumbling, spilling my ghostly drink, I struggle to my feet and apologize, saying I've got to find Zack.

Another guy gets up too. A lean, sinewy guy wearing a faded baseball cap. With a drunken start, I realize it's James Dearborn. He's by himself, just across the room. Unaccountably embarrassed, I glance away, heading for the door, stepping over people's legs. But he reaches out to grab my arm, scaring up an unexpected gust of moths in my belly.

Hold on, man. Gotta talk to you.

Disconcerted, I obey, pausing where I stand, breathing dissipated smoke. James grabs a bottle of schnapps from the arsenal of liquor on the desk. Then he leans close.

Where's Ruth?

Ruth? Uh, upstairs. Why?

Never mind. Come on.

I'm nervous, as if back in high school. We step into the sweating,

[82]

dark hallway. He worms between people; he can pry human blockages apart with his hands. Football instincts. I stay close behind, thudding into torsos, shoulders. A Portishead song is droning so loud I feel it in my testicles. We shove our way into the stairwell. Empty cups and dead cigarettes litter the stairs.

We go up to the third floor. Under our feet the floor is shaking.

Where's a place to talk, James says.

He knocks on the nearest bedroom. There's no answer, and he glances back at me. His eyes could be described as unpleasant. The irises are colored like pecans, black stains on a dark brown shell.

He tries twisting the knob: unlocked. We go inside. The bedroom is blue-silver with moonlight.

The girl who lives here has fuchsia sheets and *To The Lighthouse* is lying on top of them. I sit on the bed, which is filthy with crumbs. James lights a cigarette, and I light one, too. The place is going to smell like smoke.

Exhaling, he slumps against the wall. He's wearing an old jersey, long-sleeved, and looks gaunt.

He takes a long, punishing drink of schnapps. Dull flecks of gold float at the bottom of the bottle, and, with hidden, dark eyes, he studies me.

I gotta talk to you about something, man.

What? What's up?

Well, I debated whether I should talk to you. This kind of hits close to home. And I don't know, it might—mean something to you. You've probably already heard.

Heard?

The thing about my old coach. From school. *High* school.

(I knock glowing ashes on the rug; they disappear.)

Huh? I say.

You remember Coach Mursey?

FIRES

Yeah, of course. How come?

Okay, I guess you didn't hear, then.

James extracts from his pocket a crushed piece of paper. He carefully unfolds it. No, it's two pieces. He gives them to me.

I turn to the window to read. What I'm holding are newspaper articles—one from *The Frederick Herald,* the other from the AP wire—that he has printed off the internet. One is a week old; the other less than twenty-four hours. I read them both, which takes me a couple minutes, because I read them carefully.

Then I read them again.

Something is happening to my skin, something cold. Something hot, too. I feel it crawling over me. I sit down on the bed.

Closing my eyes, I see a strange image: the neighborhood where we grew up, outside Bondurant—but eerily rearranged, like a surrealist painting. Houses upside-down, trees bare and leafless in the summer sun, dogs shitting in swimming pools. I open my eyes. James is staring at me.

It's pretty—odd, I finally say.

Odd?

I talked to my mom today. She didn't mention anything about this.

Hm. Odd.

Yeah, no joke.

In one hand he holds the angry, smoldering Lucky Strike and in the other he clutches the neck of the schnapps. His gaze is deliberate, never leaving me.

Any thoughts?

There's a hard, knife-edged sound to his voice; he enunciates every word, forms it perfectly in his mouth, then gives it like a sacrament. And now he's waiting for an answer and I want to give the right one. But my shoulders just rise, then fall.

ANTOSCA

None? Really?

Well, *fuck*, I say. What do you want, it's a shock. If it's true. I mean, he lived right across from me.

The end of his cigarette glows red and he exhales into the silver dark.

Yeah, right across the street from you, James says with a certain persistence, as if trying to get at some detail. Saw you every day. You saw him.

Yeah. Every day.

But, so, you never saw anything?

No, of course not.

You never knew *any*thing?

No.

He looks at me as if he thinks there's something else, something I'm not telling, and if I would just be honest, he could trust me. It makes me nervous. We are children of the same place, there's an unspoken connection, and he's tugging on his end of it.

But I don't know how I'm supposed to respond, and after a moment he looks away, disappointed. I ask—Can I keep these, the articles?

Yeah. Fine.

There's a sudden, concentrated riot of embers as James stabs his cigarette out. And now he sighs slowly, like a surrender.

Listen, he says. I'm going back home tomorrow.

What? To *Bondurant*?

Yes.

Really? You're really going back?

Really.

Why?

I want to see it.

But—you can't. I mean, they're evacuating. The Appalachians are a fucking inferno. You can't get in there.

What do you think this is, *Close Encounters of the Third Kind*? With military roadblocks and shit? They're fighting a fire. They won't notice.

Well, what do you want me to say? It's a really bad idea, James.

Why?

'*Why*'?

Yeah, why, Jon? Why is it a bad idea? You sound scared.

I'm not scared, I say.

Well, me either. And I'm going. But I am kind of surprised. I thought you might feel the same way I do.

Shit, James, he was your coach, not mine. I hardly knew him.

Somehow that seems exactly the wrong thing to say, and he looks almost disgusted with me.

Whatever, he spits. Just saying.

Well, I mean—what exactly—where will you go?

I'll go to his house.

Why, man?

I want to.

But, *why*?

I want to fucking see it. I've got to see. Don't you?

What?

You can come, you know.

I don't say anything, but I think about the neighborhood that I've been to in my dreams lately, the place of grass clippings and droning lawnmowers. Involuntarily—despite what I've just read—I feel a rush of comfort, the warmth of pleasant memories. Then for a disorienting moment I hear rain—but it's only James drumming his fingers gently on the schnapps bottle. He's still looking at me, and I feel the weight of shared history, the parallel of our lives. He lights another cigarette and the bottle sloshes.

James, sorry, I—I don't want . . .

His dark shape shrugs. Alone is not always a bad thing, he says.

Tomorrow morning I'm—I'm getting on the train to Atlantic City. *That's* what I'm doing. So I won't be getting back home for like a week, at least. But maybe I'll, I'll see you around. I hope so. We can hang out. Cool?

He nods. Sure, man.

Smoke uncoils in the darkness. There are voices in the hall. They move past the bedroom and fade into the thumping roar downstairs.

We better get out of here, I say.

Yeah.

Folding the articles and shoving them in my pocket, I stand. Ruth is upstairs. (*You'll sleep here tonight, won't you?*) James drinks the last of the schnapps and tosses the bottle out the window. It shatters on the sidewalk. He moves toward the door, then stops.

Listen, he says, I know it's a little awkward. But just to say it: no hard feelings between us, okay? At least, not from my side.

Yeah, of course, I say. Of course not. Wait. I don't understand— why would there be hard feelings?

Just Ruth, he says. That's all I meant.

'Just Ruth'—just what about Ruth?

Well, *her*, you know. No resentment on my part, okay?

James, why would you have resentment about Ruth? Toward who? Me?

Well, you know. Some might say you, well, stole her from me.

Stole her? (My mind does a somersault, lands on shaky ground.) Oh, wait a second, wait just a second, man. Hold up now. *Hold up*. I don't believe this shit. It was *you*.

What was me? James asks.

The bruises. You beat her up.

I beat her up? he says, genuinely shocked.

FIRES

James is incalculably stronger than I am, but I take a step closer, facing him full on. If I had all my wits I'd be more careful, but I'm staggered, ready to fight, all good sense gone.

You gave her all those bruises, I say.

Well, yeah, he says. You know how she is.

No, tell me, James. You tell me because I guess you know. How *is* she?

Well, you know. Likes to be hit.

I bite my lip, turn to look at the wall, grimacing. Oh, man, I say.

Wait, James says, you didn't know I was with her before you?

No. I didn't.

Oh, he says. Well, I was pissed off at you for a while. And her. But I don't know. It wasn't like she was even, you know, my girlfriend.

No?

No, man. We were just kind of compatible in one way, you know. We didn't even get along.

Just in one way, huh? What, sexually, you mean?

He sighs. Don't get riled up, he says. So she likes to be hurt. Am I pretty good at hurting things? Yeah. (A silence, now. He puts a hand on my shoulder, grips it a little too roughly.) I'm serious, no hard feelings, man. You and me, lot of stuff in common, huh? You know, when two guys have been with the same person, there's a bond, you know?

I don't know about any bond, I say.

He says nothing.

We better get out of this room, I say.

You're angry.

Oh? Am I?

Look, he says. She was with me, so what? That's the way she likes it, so what? I wasn't what she really needed. I have my own demons, I don't have the cage space for hers, too. At least that's the way she sees it and I guess she's right. That brother situation, truly, I can't help with that.

That 'brother situation'?

With her brother, James says. You know.

We stare at each other, dueling it out in silence.

Right, I say. Her brother. *That* thing.

More silence. Is he laughing at me somewhere in there? Does he know I'm bluffing? I see him hurting her. He says, Let's get out of here.

Yeah.

When we go outside, two girls are huddled in the hallway, talking in quiet tones. They give us strange looks as we emerge.

What up, says James, and they don't say anything.

He disappears into the stairwell, and I resist the urge to follow. I lean against the wall, ignoring the girls' stares.

The Information

SOMEONE IS THROWING UP ON THE STAIRS. Below, the party sounds raucous, almost rancorous. The air is dank with flesh, marijuana, cigarette smoke. I enter Ruth's hall and go into her room without knocking. This girl who I thought I loved. This girl who's been keeping me in the dark. I thought she was giving herself to me; maybe she's been giving me nothing at all.

You keep *so much* from me, I say.

She's propped in bed, a bottle in her lap, absently tugging a loose thread from her sheets. It occurs to me, suddenly, that she's an alcoholic. She says, What?

I don't know you. I thought I did, but I don't. There are doors you keep locked, and I don't even know how many.

Doors, she says. I don't what you're talking about. Doors.
James, I say to her.
So? she says.
He gave you the bruises.
You know him, then, I guess, she says.
Yeah, I know him.
Oh. Yes. It was James.
So let me just—can I confirm something? You were still fucking him after we met, weren't you? You were going over there, coming back and getting in bed with me.
That was before you and I actually slept together. I broke it off with him first. That was important to me.
Her trivial, self-justifying distinction enrages me. I believe her—I can see that she isn't lying—but still I'm furious. This anger, where does it come from? I take a step forward and point my finger, about to scorch her with the full force of it, when she says softly, I don't know anything about you, either.
What? What's that mean?
It *means* I don't know anything about *you*, either.
Yeah you do. I tell you things.
Then apparently your past is nothing but a couple of amusing anecdotes. Oh, your mom caught you and your girlfriend in grandma's kitchen, huh? Well, bully for you, Jon. Because I guess other than that, you've had the perfect life. Not all of us have, though. And some things are a little less good to tell about than the story of your grandmother's kitchen.
I see. I apologize for boring you with my existence.
It's funny, she says. When I first met you, I thought you were damaged somehow. Wounded. I was attracted to that.
But now you don't think so.
Maybe it's just incompleteness.

What?

You seem hollow. You seem hollow. (She hesitates, sighing. Drunk, very drunk.) Neither of us knows who the other is, huh.

And that's the truest thing I've heard anyone say in a long time. Even as I hear it, I realize that my rage, at heart, has nothing to do with her. I brought it here with me and I carry it everywhere. It's always threatening to wake up, isn't it? What *is* it? Maybe just fear of being alone, disguised as an emotion I can inflict on someone else. And maybe that's what love is, too, just sad, self-reflexive emotional chemistry that has nothing to do with her but everything to do with me and who I am. *Who I am*. I think of the papers in my pocket and if they change things. If they alter my history.

I understand, suddenly.

In one breath I take in all the oxygen my lungs can hold. Then I exhale, carefully, like my chest is brittle. Slowly I go to her and kiss her on the forehead. She's puzzled. I turn to leave.

Jon—

At the door, I stop, look back.

It's over, isn't it, she says.

I close the door as I leave.

The party has devolved; it's in the bleary, incoherent, beer-stains-on-jeans stage. On the stereo a Johnny Cash song plays, low and menacing. I return to the bedroom where I met James. Reece says—

. . . name the dog Carlos, after my dealer . . .

The people look like zombies. My head collides with a giant paper mache butterfly hanging from the ceiling; I didn't notice it before. I go back into the hall, into the sagging crowd. My feet are wet with beer. I fight my way to the bathroom, where a line, including Alison, has formed.

Ali, you see James here like a minute ago?

FIRES

James who? I didn't—

Someone emerges from the bathroom and Alison dashes ahead of five people to occupy it—she's going to make herself vomit. A slow cry of anger rises from drunks with aching bladders.

I go down the stairs and step into the hot, stagnant night. So it's over, then.

Hunchbacks, wearing sandals and stained t-shirts, are vomiting their guts up under the elms. Someone's urinating against the building. I walk to the street, where streetlights cast weak halos. It's quiet, like the city took a Xanax.

I lean against the trunk of an elm, trying to grab the uncoiling threads of my mind. The desire to go back inside—to return to Ruth's room and mend things—grapples with a new malaise, a growing sense of drifting into foreign waters.

So I linger under the elm for a little longer, although I know where I'm going.

Across the street is an immense, windowless, white tomb made of stone. Its entrance is a tall door, receded into the façade, around which shadows gather. I stare into that darkness. Shameful, fascistic secrets.

I begin to walk. I have a hand in my pocket, worrying the pieces of paper there.

In a bus shelter, I stop to sit down. A block away, I can see the blue-red sign of the Japanese place below James's apartment. Bodies flow in and out, clutching plastic bags, white boxes. Reaching into my pocket, slow and nauseous, I extract the articles. I set them on my lap. I unfold them, smooth them out.

BONDURANT HS COACH MISSING
Students and staff baffled, concerned
by Paula Carver, Frederick Herald staff reporter

BONDURANT—Football Coach George Mursey, who led the Bondurant Cougars to three regional championships, has been missing since Thursday, police said.

When Mursey, who also teaches biology, failed to show up for work last Friday and Monday without calling in sick and didn't respond to phone messages, the school asked police to check on him.

"The house was empty and so was the garage. No one was there and there was no sign of a break-in," said deputy Mark Colin.

No neighbors reported noticing Mursey leave or seeing anything unusual, the deputy said.

"It wouldn't be like George to just leave," said BHS principal Nancy Votenka. "He takes his responsibility to students incredibly seriously. He's one of the most dependable people I've ever met."

"Our community is small," said Mursey's neighbor and BHS 10th-grader Amanda Pesta. "We're all worried. Whatever it is, we just hope he's okay so he can get back to teaching us and winning games."

Mursey's green 1994 Toyota Celica is missing as well. Police have asked anyone

> who may have seen Mursey or his car after
> last Thursday to contact them immediately at
> 301-834-7045.

I set this article aside. The second one sits beside it on my lap. I press my fingertips to my closed eyelids, causing lights to swell in the twitching darkness.

Mursey

James Dearborn was Mursey's favorite for obvious reasons: he was an incredible athlete. Any coach would have loved him. James was varsity quarterback by the end of his freshman year. He was that good. Some of the other athletes were jealous, no doubt. By 12th grade he had developed such rapport with Coach Mursey that it edged over the line between mentorship (with all its assumptions of demarcation between roles) and friendship. This was well-known in the halls of Bondurant High.

George Mursey was the best coach in our school's history. He just kept winning. And with James, the Cougars were almost unbeatable. But Mursey was strict. He didn't let players on the field unless they kept a B- average, and nobody with a D or F stayed on the roster, period. He held mandatory study sessions once a week, in which he kept the team locked in the library for two hours after school, forcing them to finish homework before the weekend.
You'd think they'd have hated him, but they didn't. With a sort of emotional black magic, he drew love from suffering.
Maybe the football players were impressed by the lack of pity underneath Mursey's big, friendly exterior. An ex-soldier tends to

have that—dangerous inflexibility in his personality, useful on the battlefield but frighteningly out-of-place in civilian life—and Mursey had been a marine in Saudi Arabia.

But one human weakness that did get through the façade was Mursey's genuine affection for James. It was the affection of an uncle for a favorite nephew, or the one-sided love of an aging ladies' man for his teenage bride.

Beginning each April, I used to mow his front yard once a week. I would see him on his porch, reading *Sports Illustrated* or *Field and Stream* or the NEA newsletter; he was a hunting enthusiast and a sportsman. His dog, a regal-looking Dalmatian named Joe Montana, sat at his side. I had to be careful, mowing, to avoid metallic signs that said things like "Protected by ADT Security" or "Neighborhood Watch."

He would go inside as I worked, and later, usually when the sun was setting, he'd reemerge with glasses of cold, sugary coffee in which ice cubes sweated and jostled, and offer me one along with my money.

One summer I worked at Ace Hardware and sometimes saw him in the store, pursing his lips and stroking back his thinning hair as he stalked the aisles, a big man, the dome of his head visible above the racks. He was always coming in to get keys made—overzealous about home security, it seemed—or to purchase pliers or chemicals or steel hinges for whatever household project he had going. He was man's man: he seemed to do a lot of pointless home fortification projects in his free time, building things, making things. He lived alone; he was divorced and had a son about my age, maybe younger, who never visited.

FIRES

    I took his AP Bio class as a sophomore. He liked to pace the front of the room, squeezing his big, athlete-gone-to-seed frame between desk and blackboard, as he talked about Golgi bodies or meiosis. He seemed like a nice guy, genial and open—if uninspired. Sometimes his lectures would drift, imperceptibly at first, into tangential explorations of some opinion or generalized viewpoint which he was a proponent of; he talked often of self-control and its "integral role" in a "well-lived life," giving as an example his own decision to quit drinking, and the discipline he had exercised in denying himself the liquor that he obsessively craved.

    Waking up at a friend's house one weekend, I slammed my face against the ladder of a bunk bed, and by Monday I had a black eye. Mursey told me to come see him during lunch.

    I slid into a desk but Mursey beckoned me forward, so I moved to the front of the classroom, nervous, and sat down. His eyes were kind and friendly, as if he was looking at a baby bird. I thought it was about my midterm grade.

    How are things, Jon? he said mildly, playing with a pencil.

    Good, I guess.

    Your grade is fine. Don't look so nervous. Coffee?

    Huh?

    Want some coffee?

    Oh—uh, no thanks.

    Nice job on the cross-country article.

    Thanks.

    I'm always impressed with your work ethic. And I don't just mean mowing my lawn. (A gentle grin as he poured coffee and handed me a cup.)

    Thank you.

    Jon?

Yeah?

I wonder if you want to tell me how you got the black eye?

Oh. I slammed it on my cousin's bunk bed.

Jon, please.

I slammed it on the ladder. It comes down right next to where your face is.

Jon, I didn't just fall off the truck.

I—Mr. Mursey, nobody hit me, if that's what you're asking. Really.

Sighing, he leaned forward and placed a hand on the arm of my chair, staring at me with his big ovaloid face. His eyes were bleached-blue. A soft, deeply pitying look crept over his features.

Hey, Jon? I'm trying to help you. Okay? Tell me if I'm wrong, but I think you need someone you can talk to. That's what you need right now. Believe me, I understand. I went through a lot as a young man, and so I understand exactly. The decisions, confusions, surprises. You don't have to tell me who did that to you. But I can help. Because I can listen. Not many adults can do that. Do you hear what I'm saying?

He leaned forward, his eyes locking into mine, and I resisted the temptation to look down. Then I noticed that a veneer of careful blandness which normally obscured the sharpness of his features was gone. There was a crystalline keenness to the man. For an instant I almost found myself trying to remember what bastard had blackened my eye.

A bell rang. Mr. Mursey, I said, you've got the wrong idea.

Hey, hey. Not everybody is against you, Jon. I want you to know I have an hour between fourth period and football practice, and I'd be more than happy to let you have that time if you ever have to get anything off your chest. Anything you say stays between you and me. Or feel free to just come across the street sometime and knock on my door. We can sit at the kitchen table, have coffee, and bullshit about life in general. Don't worry, I can be a listener instead of a teacher—today notwithstanding. (He grinned.) Okay?

The hallway was beginning to get noisy. I sat in silence for a moment. There was a sort of pleasing, unseasonable fog surrounding my thoughts. Vaguely I remembered—the bunk bed, the black eye.

I said, Thanks, Mr. Mursey. It's nice of you. But I don't really have anything to say. Then I rose and walked from the room. As I left, he said: Remember—any time.

Back in the hallway, noisy students flowed between classes. I went to my locker and got my books.

That was near the end of sophomore year, only a few weeks after my coke experience with James. It was also a time when James was becoming closer and closer to Mursey and everyone knew it. Once when I came by his classroom after school to ask a question, I found James there with him, going over football plays with him in a notebook. The season didn't start until next fall.

The team practiced in the summer, though, and by the time school started again, it seemed like James was like a close personal friend of Mursey's. And with him as captain, the football team looked like it was going to dominate for a third consecutive year.

Then in early winter, James sank into depression. His parents had divorced, or begun taking legal steps toward divorce, in August. But it wasn't until November that his personality seemed to warp under the stress. The football team began losing and James wasn't showing up at parties anymore. One night he smashed the picture windows of two houses. There was no evidence it was him, but kids knew. The football team limped into the playoffs to die, and James lost his status as Mursey's protégé, a humiliation which surely didn't alleviate his inexplicable rage.

Bus shelter

I LIGHT A CIGARETTE; the smoke tastes acrid but necessary.

Considering what I now know, that meeting in Mursey's classroom seems unimaginably perilous. At the time he was—and continued to be for many years—nothing but background scenery in the history of my life. Unassuming, humble in his ordinariness. But now I realize that things were not what I thought.

The second article:

> **BODY OF TEEN FOUND AFTER TEACHER'S DISAPPEARANCE**
> Thu May 2, 2:43 PM ET
> *by LISA BOYLE, Associated Press Writer*
>
> BONDURANT, MD - Police discovered the body of a teenage boy this afternoon in the home of a high school teacher who has been missing since last week.
>
> The unidentified body was found in a concealed room in the basement. Officers who saw the body described it as Caucasian and between 15 and 18 years old.
>
> The owner of the house, George Mursey, was declared missing on Tuesday after he failed to show up at work and police found his house empty. Mursey is a biology teacher and football coach at Bondurant High School.
>
> Police told reporters that although the boy had died recently, they believe he had been held prisoner in the basement prior to death. One

source said documents and photographs found in the house lead police to speculate that he may have been there as long as eight years.

A source within the police department said that the body showed evidence of sexual assault. Authorities said the cause of death has not been determined and they are still investigating the identity of the youth.

The discovery comes as local and state authorities are pooling resources to evacuate suburbs outside Bondurant, which lies in the path of several out-of-control wildfires that have destroyed almost five thousand acres of Appalachian forest.

Slowly, I fold both articles, put them back in my pocket. There is still time to change my mind. I could forget about going to see James. I could still turn back, try and reconcile with Ruth. But a terrible curiosity—about myself, about the history of my life, about secrets—prevents this. Is this true? Eight years. A life was happening right across the street so different from mine that feels like a refutation of it.

The past feels like now a prism now, turning the light, deceiving the eye.

In The walls

A BUS RUMBLES UP THE STREET. I get to my feet so it won't stop for me. I kick a candy wrapper off my shoe.

ANTOSCA

Walking toward James's, I feel like I'm moving across the ocean floor. Homeless men, swaying like huge stalks of seaweed, demand money. I drift down the sidewalk to a dirty door beside the Japanese place which occupies the first floor of James's building. A tenant list is posted beside the door. I hit the intercom, and a moment later I hear static.

I say loudly: It's me. Jon. Danfield.

The intercom snaps off and there's an audible click. I try the door—it opens into a small, dark vestibule. An ancient light flickers madly. I walk up the stairs, hand sliding up a stripped, dented railing, and reach a tight hallway. The apartment doors have letters, not numbers. I knock on his.

He opens it. He's wearing the same clothes, sans baseball cap—his dirty blond hair is matted to his head and doesn't look washed. He turns around and fades back into the apartment. I enter, closing the door behind me.

It's a single, taciturn room. A bed and kitchenette. The room is square. There is no overhead light, just a lamp casting piss-yellow light. Dark green wine bottles are arranged neatly on the counter. I smell ammonia and cigarettes.

Obscurely cheerful, he sits on the bed and touches his throat, like it's sore, then rests his forearms on his knees. There's blond stubble on his jaw. He kind of looks like Cupid, but grown up and venal.

I say, You're going home tomorrow?

Yeah.

You got a ticket?

I'll get one at the gate.

Beneath us, I hear the din of the Japanese restaurant. Dim, sharp voices and clattering steel. Machines thumping. But there's another noise, too, a kind of ugly, constricted rumble in the walls, like something is trying to clear its throat and will soon speak boomingly.

FIRES

James takes some pills from his bedside table. He swallows them without water.

How—I mean, how do you—expect to get into his house?

I'm sure it won't be too tough.

What about cops? It'll be a, you know, evidence scene.

We'll see.

The apartment has no A/C, and both windows are open. From the street we hear cars and pedestrians—he lives above one of the larger thoroughfares in New Haven. A bus rumbles past. Again there's a strange noise in the walls. A choked, gastrointestinal groaning.

What is that? I ask softly.

The pipes. Something broke a few months ago. You get used to it.

He rises, drifting to the kitchenette, and sinews flex under his shirt. He is in extraordinary physical condition.

The plumbing seems to be digesting itself somewhere in the wall, but I can't tell exactly *which* wall the groaning is coming from. The noise rises and abates. And again. Water roars in the sink, and I realize he's doing dishes.

Why? I ask. Tell me that again.

I want to see, he says. And there's another thing, too. I think there are—some of my things still in his house. From back when. I'd like to get them before the police do.

Steam rises from the sink. A wine bottle, half-empty, sits beside it. Dishes clatter and the walls groan. He grabs a whiskey bottle with a soapy hand and drinks from it. I sit on the bed, watching him, weighing my words. Finally I speak.

I'm going with you.

His back remains toward me.

I figured you would.

A long pause, during which the nearest wall begins to sob.

I say, Tomorrow morning, then.

ANTOSCA

Yeah.

When?

When we get up. Trains leave all day.

So I'll come over here, then? We'll go from your place?

Sure.

I put my chin on my fists and listen to the walls. Now the noises remind me whales, their deep, leviathan groaning under the waves. The lamp begins to flicker. The wall nearest me begins to vibrate, like a radiator gone insane.

That's the *pipes*? I yell.

Yeah. They *do* that sometimes.

As he says this, the thudding grows louder and is joined by a screaming, unsteady moan that makes the pane rattle in the window. I stare dumbfounded at the wall as the violence builds—something is thudding so hard the bed shakes. A spray of dust comes from the ceiling. A half-smoked cigarette jumps off the edge of an ashtray. Something in the building's intestines is about to go over the brink, to literally explode.

Then—abruptly—the noise just stops. Nothing. There's a quick papery rattle behind the wall, like a giant moth, but it stops too. James finishes washing out a bottle of wine with dish soap.

Hey, I say, one thing.

Yeah?

You know I don't know anything about Ruth's brother.

No?

You know I don't. Tell me.

Tell you about Ruth and her brother. All right. When they were little kids their parents got in some trouble. Got hooked on smack, started getting into crack. Lost their cars, almost lost their house. The mom disappeared, took all the crack and valuables in the house and ran off for good. Ruth is ten or eleven by then and taking care of Chris, the brother, who's maybe five years old. She's really fucking smart, obviously, you know this, and despite everything, she has her shit together and even at that age she's good at looking out for him. But then their dad gets busted for possession. So the state takes the kids, puts them in foster homes. At first they're together, and Ruth's still looking out for Chris. Then they get separated and she can't keep her eye on him anymore. She's twelve or so. *Her* new foster home is fine—decent family, suburbs. But her brother's is—okay, the details are sketchy. Apparently the woman wasn't even supposed to be allowed to give foster care anymore but there was some kind of paperwork error. Anyway, one night, in circumstances that aren't really clear, Chris was soaked with lighter fluid and set on fire.

What? Did he die?

Yeah, he fucking died! He was seven years old. After their dad found out, he got himself together. It took a while but he got Ruth back. By then her foster parents had got her into some private high school and she was doing pretty good. But as you can imagine there are lingering issues. For her, I mean. The guilt.

I move suddenly toward the door, as if to leave this knowledge here, with him. I reject it.

He says, You still coming with me?

I—yeah. I am.

Why?

Because I want to, I say.

Why?

I don't know.

He nods slowly, as if waiting for more. But I have nothing more to say, although he seems to expect a confession of some sort. The pipes rattle tentatively, startling me.

All right, then, I say uneasily. Tomorrow morning.

Bright and early.

ANTOSCA

I go to the door. Before I leave, I glance back. He's turned away from me, drying the dishes, and the outlines of his shoulder blades are visible under his jersey like folded, deformed wings. He has perfect posture.

I check my voicemail and find one message waiting. It's Ruth, but I can't understand a word—she's crying, maybe. Or barely conscious, close to passing out. I can almost smell the whiskey.

What now? I don't know where to go, so, feeling wretched, I retrace my steps.

The people still at the Sexplex party are glassy-eyed, dead. The dorm stairs are a dark graveyard of cigarettes and beer cans. I can feel soft, wet cigarette butts under my shoes. My heart is beating so rabidly.

In her hallway, it's dark and quiet. I feel like a burglar. I tap her door. No answer. With a twist of the knob, I go in.

She's passed out, splayed on the bed like a drowned person.

Why am I nauseous, and why does my nausea feel like guilt? I give it a minute to fade. Ruth doesn't move. Then—impulsively, shamefully—I slip fully dressed into bed with her. This must be the last time I'll ever lie next to her. What have I done? I'm shaking.

Maybe I love this girl.

She's wearing just cotton boxers, nothing else, but she is flushed and perspiring. I wish I had known. How could I blame her for anything? But it doesn't matter now, all that's irrelevant—I don't deserve her in the first place. No breeze comes in her open window. I won't go to sleep. I'll just lie here a minute, beside her, then go home to my own bed.

A little music comes from downstairs, but the voices I hear sound muted, like transmissions from a different planet.

The Beginning

AND NOW I WAKE BESIDE RUTH in the homicidal heat. Before I turn it off, the clock radio says that mountains are on fire. But I know that already. I grew up below those mountains and the image that flashes in my head is black smoke and melted toys.
    But that's not what I'm thinking about.

* * *

    Ruth is face-down in her pillow, shoulders bare. Gorgeous—and still unconscious, thank God.
    I slip out of bed as quietly as possible. A glance around her room reveals that it's littered with belongings of mine, a fungal dispersal of odds and ends, but there's nothing I need. I step into the hall, butterflies in my stomach. As I start down the stairs I can hear showers running on every floor.
    When I step outside, the sun hits me like an interrogation light. I hurry over to my dorm and go upstairs. One of the guys I live with is slouched in the common room, watching cartoons and eating Kix. He glances up, mouth full of cereal.

You leaving now?
Yeah, man. Have a good summer.
You too.
I take a shower. It doesn't take long to pack. I figure I won't need much, and I've already locked up my valuable stuff—stereo, computer—in storage. I shove socks, Tylenol, and cigarettes into my backpack. There are clothes at the house in Maryland that I can wear, so I don't need to worry about that. Hoisting my backpack, I walk back into the hall.

That's all you're taking? says the guy in the common room.
Yep.
He shrugs, and his eyes drift to the television. I walk back downstairs and go outside, back into the heat. If the city seemed like the bottom of the ocean last night, now it's the cracked landscape of a desert. Homeless people are bleached bones. I'm pouring sweat as I walk down the street. Dry, drained-out people slip past.

A bus rumbles past. I reach the Japanese place and buzz up to James's. There's a click and I go up the stairs, into the dark, sweltering hallway. I knock.

It's open.
I enter his apartment. The place is gloomy even in daylight. I notice a fist-sized dent in the far wall, where the plaster is caved in, and can't remember if it was there last night. James sits by the window, smoking a Lucky, wearing a long-sleeved shirt and dirty jeans. He's just shaved, I think, because his cherub face is smooth and speckled with blood.

Ready?
He glances at me. Yeah. You?
Aren't you gonna change? It's hot as fuck.
He sits forward. So we're gonna take the Amtrak into D.C., he says, then the MARC to Bondurant, then just walk.

Oh. Okay. Cool.

One thing, though. (He kills the cigarette on the windowsill, then tosses it to the street.) I assume—since it's across the street—we can stay at your house?

This hasn't occurred to me. It makes sense, of course. But I hesitate. The idea seems like a bad one, somehow. I shift, nervous. He shakes aspirin from a bottle.

Well?

Sure. We can stay at my place.

Great.

You're packed and everything?

Yeah. Let me finish my cigarette.

He lights another one as he says that. I sit on the bed to wait. I feel the heat rising with the day. A groaning emanates from the walls, then cramped silence.

I search for a mundane topic of conversation. Finish your finals all right? I ask.

He looks at me strangely. I didn't have any, he says. I'm not enrolled.

What?

I'm not enrolled anymore.

What? Since when?

Since I decided not to take any credits this semester. You're only allowed to take two semesters of leave though, and I already used up both of them.

You've dropped out? I ask, hiding incredulity.

Huh. I guess you could call it that.

Then what are you still doing here?

Oh. Just living here. You know.

He lapses into silence and leans back in a fakery of nonchalance. The light is coming from behind him and makes his face hard to see.

There are two windows in the apartment and they're beside each other. Each is a bath of sunlight, but the brightness seems to drain from the light when it enters the room, where it is strained and yellowy like an old sepia photograph. James sits against the wall in the dark space between the windows. He's part of the shadow, a big woolly darkness draped over him, and I remember warm rain and a half-built house, and I remember him across years, a different person.

Finally he finishes his second cigarette and tosses it, too, out the window. He bares his teeth at me, for some reason, and then stands, hefting a backpack. I hear the dull thud of bottles insulated in t-shirts.

Let's go, he says.

We go out into the hall. He locks his apartment.

Obscene doesn't begin to describe the heat. It's a five block walk to the station.

Lines clog the ticket counter. By the time we reach the ticket agent, the 11:30 train's filled. James pays with cash for the next one, buying both our tickets before I know it. I'll get you back, I say. I just have to go to the ATM.

Forget it.

I shrug, feeling indebted. We walk to the boarding area, where we sit and wait, and people around us read magazines, talk on cell phones. Some young boys have got a plastic doll whose eyes they're prying out.

A girl who looks like a freshman drifts over, pretending to browse a magazine rack, waiting for us to flirt, but James doesn't seem to notice, and I just look away. Finally, frustrated, the girl moves away.

My cell phone vibrates, and I dig it out.

Yeah?

Hi, dear.

FIRES

Mom.

Just wanted to make sure you didn't sleep in and miss the train. Are you on it now?

Listen, Mom—uh, I just have a minute, but there's a change of plans.

A change?

I'm not coming to Atlantic City yet—I'm driving up to Vermont, with Ruth.

Oh. For how long?

Ah, just a few days, I think. I'm not really sure. Just to meet her parents and, you know, go, uh, hiking.

Hiking?

Well, you know. Vermont.

I see.

And then I'll just come back down—okay? I'll either come to Atlantic City, if you guys are still there, then drive back home with you, or else I'll come straight back home if you're there already. If they get the fire under control by then.

Well. Okay. You're staying at her house, I guess? Her parents' house?

Uh, yeah. But you can call my cell, I don't have her number on me. Listen, Mom, I gotta go—we're in traffic. Okay? Love you. See you in a couple days. Bye.

Bye, dear, I love you—

Putting the phone away, I glance at James. There's a blankness in his eyes. I recognized nothing of the guy I knew in high school. What the fuck happened to him? This mental tangent unexpectedly blossoms into a wider, full-blown reminiscence: I miss Bondurant.

I can almost smell the chlorine, the suntan lotion, the leaves burning somewhere down my street. I see glitter flickering down on the homecoming parade. I smoke weed on wet, confetti-strewn bleachers, late at night.

[110]

I think about the fires and what they'll destroy.

Everyone gets to their feet. The doors open, the train is boarding. We follow the crowd up concrete stairs and into the nightmare heat. Filing onto the train, I get goose bumps. The air conditioning is arctic. We find seats and throw our backpacks into the overhead storage and then we sit, saying nothing, and soon the doors close and we creep toward Maryland.

Eyes Closed

ON THE TRAIN I AM THINKING ABOUT THE WILDFIRES.

I see dry lightning storms and discarded cigarette butts setting the world on fire. I see news footage of fires that have become massive, insane, godlike things. Heavy winds send them leaping for miles, from tree to tree, house to house. Mountainsides disappear. At a certain point, the monster loses any hesitation it once had, any vulnerability, and it attacks middle-class homes, melting them and gnawing them, boiling the water in backyard pools.

At the edge of my neighborhood there is a flat, lonely cornfield which belongs to a farmer who, years ago, wouldn't sell his land to developers. On the other side of that field the land begins to rise, and suddenly you are not in the suburbs anymore, but on the mountain.

The Appalachians don't get a lot of fires. The vegetation isn't as dense or dry as it is in the Southwest, and the old, eroded Appalachians are not mountainous like the Rockies. In states that get big fires every year there are efficient, perfected systems to fight them. Not in Maryland. The system is rusty and the firefighters aren't experienced. This is a bad thing for the subdivision called Copper Creek Estates which sits now at the foot of a burning mountain, a cluster of cool, airy homes flanked by sagging maples and shrubs that are turning crisp and khaki-tan. It is a close-knit, pleasant neighborhood just outside of Bondurant. The houses are close together, so you never feel alone or far from neighbors. Sometimes at night, the maple branches tap the windows.

Getting close

I WATCH ENDLESS, endless stands of withering trees slide past the window. Beside me, James sleeps, knotty hands curled in his lap.

Two little blond girls dash up the aisle, chasing each other and fighting over a damaged doll. Other passengers sleep, heads askew at odd, heavy angles. I stare at the mountains in the west, over which the sun gleams like a hot bronze eye. Our little toy train bustles down the east side of the continent.

Getting up, I go to the dining car and buy a cranberry juice and a chicken sandwich in a bag. I sit and eat alone. After a while I go back and edge past the still-dozing James. He reeks of tobacco.

The train rattles over marshes; we are so close to the pools of water that we must be on raised tracks. In the distance I see the gray, lilac silhouettes of the Appalachians.

Where is Ruth? She's on a train headed north—and if she looks out her window, she can probably see the Appalachians too, pale blue-violet phantoms on the horizon. Peaceful heaps of dead ghosts or gods, piled end to end on the edge of the world. I think of Ruth, undressed, lying amid crumpled sheets that are damp from our sweat.

James bares his teeth in his sleep.

I wake him as we ease into Union Station.

We haul our backpacks down from the overhead rack and walk onto the platform.

As people stream off the train, we stand in the late-afternoon heat and smoke cigarettes, drawing dirty looks from the better-dressed passengers, and then we walk into Union Station to wait for the next MARC. Sitting listlessly in the air conditioning, James plays with his lighter as a guy with a tracheotomy watches him without expression.

The train arrives. People rise, shouldering bags and backpacks, and trundle out to the platform. The MARC is small. We step inside and find seats; James gets one by the window. Soon the train starts to move. The city turns into patches of dry forest.

The Appalachians are still visible, and now for the first time, I can see smoke. It does not look malevolent; it's nothing but a blister of gray on the mountainside. James sees it too and stares without speaking, his reflection barely visible in the window.

As we pass through the woods, we lose sight of the mountains, and James turns to me.

You scared?

Of the fire?

No, man, of the *dark*. Yeah, the fire.

Not really. I mean, it might make me a little anxious once we get there.

Uh-huh.

You don't care at all, do you?

Oh, I care.

He lapses into contemptuous silence. The daylight dwindles, its absence nourishing shadows between trees, and an orange, hellish light appears in the sky.

So what did you leave in his house? I ask.

What?

What's the stuff of yours you want to get from Mursey's house before the police find it? That you left there?

Just some *stuff*, he says angrily, sitting back. Shrugging, I look out the window again.

A distant helicopter crosses the thin, ragged strip of visible sky—suddenly, I glimpse deer among the trees. Five or six of them wading knee-deep in the undergrowth, grazing unhurriedly, glancing up as the train roars by. Then they're gone.

Deer, I say with childish happiness.

Huh?

I saw deer.

Good for you.

And now the sparse dry trees with their shadows and black-eyed deer slip away and vanish, giving way to suburbia, a rolling eastern landscape that stretches out into the distance, a sea of lawns and driveways, and I see an endlessly unraveling panorama of houses with black asphalt tongues and azalea beards, and lazy, new roads winding this way and that through the neighborhoods. The grass is trimmed and the lawns are landscaped and dogs hover restlessly within the bounds of invisible fences. Blue swimming pools glitter under the sunset, whose orange tentacles are resting wrathfully a fingernail's distance above the smoking mountains.

I sink back in my seat, sighing, wondering if my parents enjoyed today at the beach. And if Ruth reached Vermont safely. And if Coach Mursey is dead, or maybe heading for Mexico. I wonder where his dog is now, the big Dalmatian called Joe Montana, and I wonder if squirrels are gathered on the grass outside my dorm, and I wonder if Ruth's Barbie dolls sleep peacefully in their mass grave.

Grocery Store, Neighborhood

No one gets off with us. We walk down off the platform, into the parking lot, where a faint breeze touches us—bad news for firefighters. I haven't been back to Bondurant in almost a year; I spent Christmas at a friend's house in Guilford, Connecticut. That neighborhood was actually a lot like Bondurant, though, so I never got homesick. Before we got here I thought the air would smell like smoke. But if it does, that smell is hidden under an odor of cars and fast food wrappers and motor oil.

What is *that*? James says, looking at the outline of downtown buildings against the sky.

What's what?

That. The building bigger than all the other buildings.

Town *hall*? Dude, that's like, not new.

I haven't been back to Bondurant in almost four years.

You serious?

Summer after high school was the last time.

Damn.

For a moment we stand in silence. I sense growing, shrouded irritation on his part.

Well? he says. Let's walk.

You hungry?

I could eat. He readjusts the heavy backpack on his shoulders; again I hear the soft clank of bottles.

We walk across the parking lot. Downtown Bondurant is quiet. A headline on a discarded newspaper catches my eye ("Three Students Allege . . .") but I don't stop to read it. On a green bench outside the liquor store, a janitor I recognize from high school is scratching a lotto ticket, and beside him a red nylon leash weds a mastiff to a parking meter.

FIRES

People are walking, loitering, laughing. Before we arrived, I imagined Bondurant a ghost town—but that's ridiculous. These people aren't in any danger, except maybe from dirty air. A forest fire can't eat a town, a place of asphalt and concrete and glass. What it *can* destroy are suburbs.

We walk around a traffic circle, then trudge up a sloping lawn in front of an apartment complex. Downtown Bondurant lies behind us now; no more sidewalks. The western sky glows a malignant orange and the east is deepening into soft, sleepy blue. Ahead is the deathlike neon of the shopping center.

Dripping sweat, we reach the half-empty parking lot. Lonely shopping carts are stranded against curbs. Kids emerge from the video store, laughing in the fresh dusk.

What do you want to eat?

All the same to me. I don't even know what all's here anymore. I don't have much cash. Not Domino's, their cheese is funny.

Lotus Garden?

I hate chopstick food.

The grocery, then? And just get whatever?

That's cool.

We cross the parking lot, and go inside. The deli at the back sells hot food à la carte, and I get chicken wings with steamed vegetables and bottled water. James has a bunch of coleslaw and a hard-boiled egg.

The sky is pale blue with streaks of orange when we emerge, and soft voices come to us on the breeze. We sit on the curb and eat. In the ripening dusk, a distant curl of smoke is visible. Faint sirens come from town, and twilight gathers like a tide. The street lights flicker to life.

And as we sit, scraping last bits of food out of the styrofoam containers, I watch people cross the asphalt, going to their cars or to rent videos or buy cigarettes at Rite Aid. No one hurries. A sense of calm, of pleasantry, hangs in the damp, pastel air.

We throw our empty containers away and start walking. The grocery is near the edge of Bondurant, where suburbs and farmland collide with town, and Copper Creek Estates is about two miles away.

The shopping center sits on a high point of land, and as we stand for a moment at the edge of the parking lot, we can see much of the town. The homes are quiet and their windows glow.

In the east, our library is visible, picture window cozy with light. On the playground beside it, the swing sets are silhouettes. In the west, under a silk-covered setting sun, we can see the football field where George Mursey coached. A black V of birds crosses the sky; dogs are barking somewhere.

We set out across the access road that passes the grocery. Soon we're walking past flower gardens and driveways.

This is the sea of lawns that I saw from the train. It was forest, once, I guess, then farmland, and now it is gardens and three-car garages: the new American frontier. Sprawl.

In the air there's soft perfume of grass clippings and gasoline. Gentle electricity seems to pulse around us, and I imagine power lines below our feet and silent jets etching lines on the sky, heading south to Dulles. Then I imagine this lackadaisical geography destroyed by the fury of nature.

Gray twilight becomes the first blue feelers of night. This area hasn't been evacuated; we see lamp-lit windows and silhouettes. The soft chatter of a legion of TVs reaches us on the breeze, and we smell smoke.

We abandon the road, begin cutting across backyards, past swing sets and satellite antennae that sprout like black toadstools. We pass the house where I took piano lessons for two years. We encounter affable, barking Labradors and Chesapeake Bay retrievers, who beg us

FIRES

to cross their invisible fences and play with them. We skirt real fences that protect black, glassy swimming pools.

There's another half mile to go, and, tired and winded, I'm about to suggest a few minutes' rest, preparing even to offer James one of my cigarettes as an incentive—but now, as we emerge from the no-man's-land between two houses, we can finally see the fire.

The mountains loom over the town like village elders, but tonight there's a red, weeping sore on the nearest one. It is magnificent and awful, like a chasm has opened on the mountainside and hell is gloating there. The actual blaze is visible, flames violent against the darkness, and it's *close*, near the foot of the mountain already, descending, eating its way to our world. This fire does not look half-hearted, either. It's an inferno.

We cross the street and cut across more backyards.

And then, seemingly without warning, it is laid out before us—the neighborhood where we grew up. Stopping on its edges, I have a mutinous feeling in my heart, my nerves, my scrotum. A feeling that this is a place I have never been before. It hides here in the shadow of the mountains, leafy and complacent, containing its secrets. And it does have secrets; it is full to bursting with them. It is *ripe* with them.

We walk on.

Fine, imperceptible ash floats in the air, carried on a soft breeze, and I realize I've got the mountain in my lungs. Our neighborhood is deserted. Forgotten sprinklers have come on, making their hushed rattle all around us, like a thousand snakes hidden in dry grass—or perhaps they were left on deliberately, a pathetic defense against the fire. Garage doors are down, windows dark. And everything is like I remember, but eerily different.

The dry maples rustle; there are many of them, heavy with leaves turning brittle months ahead of time. Brown patches disfigure lawns. We come to the street where I live.

Hold on.

I glance over at him. He's frozen, tense. What's up?

Shh. Cop car.

There's a blue-and-white cruiser parked in front of Mursey's house. The cruiser is dark and appears empty. Better not to take risks, though. We slip off the road and kneel in the grass.

Then I glance at James and realize it's not the cop car. Something just struck him like a nail gun firing into his chest: he's staring at the Mursey house. His skin has gone tight over his skull.

I look back at the house. Except for the yellow police tape crisscrossing the front door, it looks normal, terrifyingly normal. He lived there with his wife, for a while—before she took their son and left. And after that, the neighbors pitied him, and his wife and son never visited, and he lived alone. Rumors started that his wife had gone off with another man, which made everyone feel even worse. Coach Mursey kept the house in good shape. He coached and taught; kids liked him and their parents admired him, and when it snowed, he shoveled the Amhersts' driveway, because Don Amherst had arthritis at forty. All this before I was even in middle school. So there it sits, in the darkness: a solid, well-kept house.

Let's go, murmurs James. His face has lost years and he looks young and scared.

Around back? he says. Just to play it safe?

Yeah.

We retreat into the nearest backyard, where a swimming pool glimmers, cloaked in shadow, and a sprinkler tosses white, wet jewels through the darkness. We cut into another yard, ducking under the dry branches of trees, and then we're in my yard. Even in darkness it is desperately, affectingly familiar, like I was here last night: the sloping lawn, the black stalk of the hummingbird feeder, the dark, boxy hulk of the deck. These are things I see in dreams. Two perfect pale images of the curved moon hang in the glass patio doors, like tired eyes.

Shit, I'll have to go around front, I whisper. I forgot I don't have this key, I can't unlock the glass doors. You go up on the deck and I'll come through the house and let you in.

He shifts the backpack on his shoulders and hurries up the stairs, and I go around the side of the house. I almost bump into the garden hose, which is coiled and hanging; it looks like a swollen black wheel in the darkness. I go into the front yard. The cop car's still sitting across the street. I go up on the porch and fumble with my backpack, find the keys, unlock the door. And then I slip inside.

I stand quite still, letting my eyes adjust. The air conditioning, which my parents have left on, is a narcotized hum.

Unexpected butterflies fill my stomach. I have the sensation of being in a museum.

It seems necessary to move with deference—with something like respect for the dead. Husks of me exist here, and if I move carelessly they may turn to dust.

On my left the stairs rise, a staggered blur in the darkness, and beside them the dining room gapes, a black cavern. I glide down the hall; in the kitchen, the moon is gleaming on the steel sink. Pearly light gathers on the counter.

I drift into the living room, where darkness is gilded navy and ivory. The glass doors welcome a wall of moonlight.

James's silhouette hovers on the other side of the glass, restless. I sense his desire to come inside, as if he fears something out there. I cross the dark living room and unlock the doors. He comes in on a gust of warm, smoky air.

Home sweet home, I say.

We go into the hall. The world is full of silent darkness. He slings off his backpack, turning. In the darkness he is charcoal-dark shadows, undefined, his eyes in patches of gloom.

Want food? I ask. If there's anything in the fridge?

Not hungry.

You all right, man?

Huh. Yeah. My head's pounding.

I hear him rummage in his backpack: the clank of bottles, pills rattling, a soft rustle of clothes. He pulls something out.

Let's drink.

All right. In the dining room.

Where?

Down here.

He follows me down the hall to the dining room. The chairs squeak on the hardwood floor.

Keep the lights off.

I fucking know that, Jon.

He sighs. I hear pills rattle again, and the bottle gurgles as he washes them down with a long drink.

What are we drinking?

Bourbon.

I take crystal glasses from the cabinet. They thud on the oak table. As he fills them, I open the curtains, bathing the room in mottled darkness, giving us a view of the house across the street.

I sit at the table. He drinks the bourbon like apple juice and refills his glass; slivers of light swirl in the bourbon.

I can, uh, smoke in here, right, Danfield?

I'm about to say no from instinct. But less than a mile away the mountain is burning, and the air outside is filled with ashes, and a Lucky Strike in my parents' dining room won't make any difference.

I say, Of course.

We take out cigarettes and I light mine off his (a kiss by fiery proxy) and then he breathes gray air at the curtains.

FIRES

The Mursey house is dark. So strange to think that it's a crime scene—which will, of course, be destroyed along with everything else if the fire comes down from the hills and begins to eat. I think about the kid who was a prisoner there, whose whole history is that basement. The fire will destroy that, too.

You ever been in that house? James asks.

I just cut the grass.

He doesn't respond. He seems disappointed.

A couple moments pass and he drinks more. I'm looking at the window, at the house across the street. I see something on the lawn which could be a dead crow or a meeting of shadows. James licks his lips.

Let's drink, he says. Let's drink to something.

Let's do.

To Ruth.

No. Something else.

No? You don't want to drink to your girl? Oh, you don't want *me* to drink to her.

I broke up with her, I say. Before I left. It's over.

He stares at me for a moment. Well, fuck her, then, he says. To the fire!

To the fire.

playground

LET'S GO OUTSIDE, he says.

Now?

Soon. Tonight.

I shrug. Why?

I want to. This is the first time I've been here in so long, man.

Fair enough, then.

Bourbon gurgles as he pours. He's already drunk twice what I have, but he doesn't seem drunk, and there's deliberateness in the way he's watching me. Still I sense a certain ebbing of control in his personality. A loosening of emotion, like something breaking away from a riverbank.

His eyes, like dark, mechanical eyes in a doll's head, roll sideways and stare out the window.

A dog is wandering out there on the street, a gigantic black dog, and it's carrying a boy's shoe in its jaws. The dog shambles past our house, lazy and slow, almost drugged, and it drops the shoe, then possessively picks it up again. Deep in my brain, a childish and unformed terror billows up and I feel small bumps rise on my flesh.

I set my glass down. And I'm shaking. Behind Mursey's house, an eerie, washed-out redness stains the horizon.

You know, James says, I used to wander out there sometimes. Alone at night.

The stars glimmer, smeared. The black dog moves out of sight.

We take the bourbon into the hall. I'm unnaccountably nervous. I'm having vague thoughts of locking James out, or maybe walking back to the train station on my own.

Ready? I ask.

Cigarettes and booze, check.

Let's—let's go, then.

Reckless, we open the door. Warm air rolls over us, grasps us— soothing me, like a subtle dark injection of heroin—and we can smell real smoke again. Not the puny, squirrelly odor of cigarettes, but the smell of burning trees. As we cross the lawn, droplets tossed by the sprinkler glitter like Mardi Gras beads. The sky smolders a glorious blue-black; keen stars glint in its folds.

FIRES

We stand on the grass, staring at Mursey's house and the empty cop car, and then James says hoarsely, Come on.

Our shoes hit the road with flat noises. The darkness and silence of the deserted suburbs are, on some level, deeply unnerving in their *wrongness*—but also comforting, calming, in a fundamental way. And I'm getting drunk now, sedated. We step off the road and cut between two houses.

Hold up, grunts James.

His dark figure slides away, blending into the shadow of a house. I hear him pissing against the porch, and then he comes back, zipping up, and we start walking again, sharing the bourbon. The hushed darkness is huge and calm. On the mountain, smoke is visible; its roots are red-stained.

Where you want to go?

Down the street.

Not far away, a dog begins barking. James drinks more bourbon. So do I. We walk past trees that rustle pleasantly. I am reasonably successful in not thinking about how alone we are.

We walk, we walk, wandering, like kids off school with nothing to do. We're on asphalt again. James stops, and after a moment, I realize he's looking at a house down the street. Confused, I follow his stare, and realize where we are.

At his driveway, we stop.

Where are they? I ask.

Gone away, he says. My dad doesn't live here anyway. He just comes by to pick up stuff sometimes.

We stand there, smelling like bourbon, looking at the dark windows, the wide porch: there it is, and because it is like all the other houses in this neighborhood, it is a lot like *my* house—and a lot like Coach Mursey's, too. A few things are different—colors, brickwork, windows—but all these places are essentially the same.

ANTOSCA

And as we pass the bottle back and forth, I realize that I want to go inside—there are histories in there, secret histories drifting loose. In the air, the empty spaces. These houses are museums. I want to go in, walk around, touch the artifacts.

Come on, he says sharply, let's get the fuck out of here.

And so we start walking again. He slips off the road and I follow him across neat, rectangular lawns. All the sprinklers are on, an endless wet gauntlet. Our cuffs grow damp, and our cigarettes glow like lazy red eyes.

Up there's the playground.

Yeah.

Let's get on the swings.

Heh. Yeah.

Our shoes crunch gravel. We walk onto grass and the shadows around us are fertile with memory. A jungle gym, a seesaw, slides. They're grim and abandoned, lonely. The ghosts of our former selves play in the dark.

I step through a sandbox, among half-buried toys. A little boy's cap lies flat in the sand, as if he's down there too. I walk across the grass, stomping sand off my shoes, thinking of Atlantic City. Ruth lying on the hot beach—and like a wave breaking over me I feel a rush of desire; I want to be with her between crisp white sheets, undressed. I want to tell James every detail about when I was with Ruth, relive it for myself and also make him jealous.

He leans against an aluminum playground slide, face all dangerous angles. Pills rattle as he fumbles in his pocket. He takes out an orange RX bottle, which I think for a moment has weed in it, but he pours white tablets, hardly visible in the darkness, into his cupped palm. He sends them to his stomach on a river of bourbon.

What were those?

Oxycodone. Painkillers.

FIRES

What hurts?

He stares off into the neighborhood. His cigarette glows as he taps ashes away, leaning against the dented, silvery slide.

I'm just tense.

He says it like it explains everything. He's *tense*. The word hangs in the air—I imagine it leaves a bitter taste on his tongue. Tossing his cigarette away, he starts to add something.

When I said it was just—

The grass crackles, and heavy, wild footsteps pound the dirt—a sudden, maddened eruption in the darkness behind us. We spin, choking on our hearts, and a thing that looks like solid darkness gallops off into the night, thudding.

Shit—

Shit—look out—

We try to penetrate the dark with our eyes. There's nothing. Houses crouch in the night; jungle gyms and seesaws are half-visible and drowned in shadow. We're poised to bolt if the thing comes back. But then hooves thud further off—there's a sound of something getting trampled. Then it's gone.

The fuck was *that?*

Looked like a fucking horse. A fucking *unicorn*.

Fuck, it was *huge*.

Unnerved, we move across the playground to where it was: near two plastic stallions on brass springs, their saddles worn down by young cowboys. The grass is torn up and flattened, but in the dark we can't find tracks. We hover, finding our breath. The plastic stallions sit on coiled springs, impassive and smug, as if *they* were the ones that tore up grass and scared the hell out of us. I have an unpleasant feeling of being in the wilderness. Huge things prowl in the suburban night.

Now James sighs a great slow gust of bourbon breath, turns back, and begins methodically looking for the bottle. He dropped it somewhere. So we search the ground, finally finding it hidden in shadows, coated in mulch. As he drinks, I stare out at the empty houses, smelling wood smoke.

Where you want to go now? I ask. Back home?

No. No, not yet.

James hands me the bottle, encouraging me to drink more, which I do.

Want to go to your house? I ask.

No. Let's go down Evergreen.

All right.

Under The Fire

I'M REALLY FEELING THE BOURBON by the time we reach the cul-de-sac. Beyond it is a wide metal gate, and beyond that is private property—a big dry cornfield that, years ago, a farmer refused to sell. So the developer built around it. Beyond the cornfield, the mountain begins to rise.

We climb onto the rusted gate, looking over cornstalks whose leaves are drooped and dry, and we light cigarettes and James drinks more bourbon. Hard to tell how drunk he is.

Above us the fire burns. We can't see flames from here—just a wall of smoke that, where it touches the mountain, is ghastly, pale red—but we can *hear* the fire. Ocean in a seashell. The threat looks terrifyingly close (even with the cornfield and the trees in our way, we could reach the flames in twenty minutes) and it's fucking huge.

Bourbon and smoke make my tongue feel like one large wound. I can taste blood in my saliva, and I spit at the dark, dry corn. A mountain's in my lungs.

I hate this place, James says.

FIRES

You can't really hate a place like this. It's too benign.
I *hate* it.
He takes a long drink, looking into the darkness. I think being here has knocked something loose in his head—and whatever it is, it's rolling around in there, knocking other things loose.
It's benign, yeah. All those years. Right across the street from your house, Danfield.
What the coach did is an exception. If it's even true, it's an exception. You know that just as well as I do.
It's a human sacrifice, that's what it is.
It is an exception, you know it is. I mean, if there's a problem, it's not a problem *with* this place. This is a peaceful neighborhood in a peaceful place. If there's a problem, it's with fucking human nature, so, you know, don't blame human nature on suburbia.
God, that fucking *faggot*. All that time . . .
Hey, I lived right across the street, I say, the alcohol making me voluble. *I* didn't know. There was no *way* to know. He seemed just like everybody else. *You* know that.
Yeah.
But you're right, it does change things. When you think about it. I mean, everything that happened during our lives here, everything we remember—all that time, right across the street . . .
Yeah.
That kid was down in that basement when we were freshmen. He was down there during our senior prom. Our graduations. All those memories, they're a little different now. Just a little, like, stained at the edges.
Uh-huh. Different.
You go through life and memory has to be—*compartmentalized*, I guess, so things can't bleed into each other.
Is that what you do? he asks, looking at me closely. 'Compartmentalize'?

ANTOSCA

Yeah. Right? You do. But this thing—it's so *close*. It's so close to the history of our lives that it bleeds over a little, you know?

James stares at the corn. He looks almost—disappointed. My font of drunken philosophy dries up, and I am suddenly embarrassed.

When you think back on it, I say hollowly, I guess you just have to remind yourself—nobody knew.

You went over there, he says. You didn't know?

Went over where? What?

To his house.

I didn't go over there. I—I mowed the lawn. I never went in the house.

What time? he asks. What time did you cut the grass?

What *time*?

What time of day.

Uh. The afternoon. I guess.

You never went in the house.

No.

Well let me tell you, he says. Let me tell you what he did with me. It was just for a few weeks that fall. Then it was over, then he let me go, and you know what? I was hurt. I was jealous. I was like a jealous girlfriend. You know what I did?

He looks at me. You know what I did? I watched his house. Midnight to 5 AM, lots of nights. I saw other guys coming out of that house. You hear me? Guys from school. *I saw other guys leaving his house.* (He is looking at me carefully—I think he believes that maybe I saw these other guys, too, that I knew something about all this back then. Is he accusing me?) Maybe I don't have to tell you what went on in there. Maybe you already know those details.

James drinks—he drinks the equivalent of four or five shots, easy, and I'm thinking that if I'd drunk as much as he has tonight, I'd have passed out long ago.

How would I know? I ask.

FIRES

You never went in that house.

James, I have *never been in that house.*

Somebody told you then, maybe. Somebody who knows. Somebody *I* told. (Anger spirals up, uncontrolled, in his voice.) Who used me.

Who? Are you talking about—Ruth?

I hear a rustling in the corn; some small animal dashing among the stalks. James drinks.

James? I thought you and Ruth—I thought it was just once. A long time ago. Right?

Am I back here again? he says. Am I here, is this real?

James? Answer me.

I hope it does burn.

Well, it might.

He exhales a long stripe of pale smoke at the stars and drinks viciously. The bottle's almost empty. I don't know how he's still conscious.

Memory's a funny thing, he says.

Um, I guess.

I remember high school. I remember *you*. Wanting to be me. A lot of people wanted that. I loved that.

James.

But look now, how things change. You don't want that anymore. Why would you? You've got something I just don't have.

Ruth isn't a thing.

That's not what I'm—fuck it.

I light a cigarette and glance at him, at his sullen silhouette. The silhouette drinks. Dry stalks of corn rustle like the skeleton of a giant, dried-up anemone.

You have a certain mental skill I lack, James says. It will help you live a long life and a sort of happy one.

Okay.
Grandkids.
Grandkids?
Me, I don't want to be around that long.
No?
Patronizing fuck.
Come on. Everybody *thinks* about it.
Almost nobody *really* thinks about it.
Why? I ask. Did you?
The fire makes a low, endless animal noise.
Tell me, I say.
Ha—tell you. He laughs abruptly, not a sardonic laugh but a giggle, accompanied by a facial transformation from hate to innocence—but then it drains, leaving his face dark and strange again.
How did you do it? I ask.
Oh, ha ha, this is a good story. The first time? Or the second? I don't know . . .
A dense pause, and when finally he begins to talk, it's almost like he's mocking me with it.
Well, the second time, he says, I was a sophomore—at college, I mean. I don't know, I just took a bunch of vicodin and some vodka, nothing fancy. I just underestimated my tolerance. Woke up covered in piss and vomit and couldn't walk, my muscles were basically spaghetti. When I realized I was still alive, I just kind of sighed.
Shit.
First time, freshman year, that was a little more serious. Cancelled my credit cards, closed my bank account, everything. I planned it all. I had a knife in my room and a bucket of ice water. And—
You couldn't do it.
He flips over his right arm and pulls up the sleeve, displaying his forearm—bas-relief veins—and I see a white scar that climbs to the hollow of his elbow.

FIRES

You *did* it?

Then I lost my nerve.

Now he exposes his left arm, tugging up the sleeve to reveal untouched flesh. He rotates it, both ways, to convince me there are no scars.

See? See that? That's failure to act. And it's fucked up my life on more occasions than one.

What happened then? When you lost your nerve?

I started to panic. I got *really cold*.

You called 911.

Fuck no. I made a bandage with socks and packing tape, and then I held my arm over my head. My whole side cramped up—it was pretty horrible. I started hallucinating.

Shit.

I was pretty disappointed in myself.

You ever tell anyone this?

James pauses. No.

Emphasizing this with a shake of the head, he glares down at his shoes, which rest on the bars of the gate. His silence seems precarious. The dry corn rustles. He sighs, and a few words escape.

Ruth guessed, obviously.

She did?

The scars, man.

The distant silhouette of a fruit bat dances against the thick, gray-red tendrils of smoke, like a gnat trapped in a lantern. Beside me, James looks fragile. When his arm slashes up to hurl the bourbon bottle into the cornfield, I flinch. Dry leaves crackle and the bottle crashes somewhere in the dark rows.

We should probably—go soon, I say limply. Back to the house.

Hm.

But we could smoke another cigarette first, if you want.

Hm.

As I take out my cigarettes and give him one, a dog starts to bark nearby, startling me. What the hell are all these dogs doing here? Did their owners leave them? The cornfield rustles eerily.

I said I'd tell you what he did to me, James says.

Yeah.

But I wouldn't know where to begin.

Oh.

I feel like I might be sick.

All right.

He doesn't get sick, though. He just sits there, letting smoke seep out of his nostrils. I have the uncanny feeling that something insane is going to happen, he's going to burst into flame or something. Nothing happens.

It's unnerving, the intensity of his rage, and I want nothing more than to get back to the safety of the house.

Let's get out of here.

Yeah, in a minute.

A warm breeze comes down the mountain, bringing ashes and a smell of barbecued leaves. I watch the fire; the eastward wind keeps it maddened, alive. It crackles up there on the mountainside, barely a half-mile off. And I remember the night I spasmed awake next to Ruth, burning up from a dream where something hunted me.

Kitchen

BY THE TIME WE GET BACK, I know something's different. Walking home he's been silent, vibrating with kamikaze anger. He's been walking ahead of me, as if I'm not here.

FIRES

We go inside, into the kitchen. He begins to pace back and forth in the sea-dark shadows. His movements are unsteady, miscalculated.

A new cigarette glows, clamped between two of his fingers. He goes to the fridge and takes out a gallon jug of water. He drinks in gulps, pausing for breath.

Then he goes into the bathroom and I hear him urinating, an endless flat noise. He doesn't flush. He comes back to the kitchen. In his expression and the hardness of his eyes there is nothing to make contact with.

punishment

I DON'T WANT TO BE ALONE. When he goes to the dining room, I follow. He's furious about the cornfield, I think—furious at me for witnessing his loss of control, his self-loathing.

He sits at the table, digging his fingernails insolently into the oak finish. Shadows cover him like black algae. The air conditioning hums, a relentlessly indifferent sound, and I sit across from him.

You gonna sleep?

He doesn't reply. His cigarette glows; the drink gleams in his glass.

We could watch TV. Or something. Just to kill time.

Nah. Let's arm wrestle, he says. Best two out of three.

Arm wrestle?

Yeah, come on, man. Let's *bond*.

Uh, okay.

Dropping his cigarette in a vase—it hisses, water at the bottom—he slides his drink aside. I'm well aware that I'm going to lose. I want him to win.

We clasp. The pain is sudden and precise. He pulverizes my hand, folding it back on my wrist like a locket—then he's bending my elbow back, slower than necessary (I'm barely resisting, just sort of watching from a distance), and grinding my hand into the oak so brutally I hear each knuckle crack. I see his teeth.

The instant he lets go, I'm on my feet. Backing away, rattled, making no effort to salvage my dignity. I don't want it. I just want to be sure he's going to stay where he is. The attack has left me off-balance. He is motionless in the darkness. My hand feels like a glove full of tomato pulp.

Have we bonded? he says. Are we buddies? Can we tell each other our secrets now?

Sure, James—sure.

I'm sensing you don't mean that. Go again?

I think not, I say shakily.

But I'm careful, I don't say anything else. Or make any sudden moves. I feel like there's a Rottweiler sitting there, lips curled, and I have to be very cautious.

Ruth

My hand throbs. In the upstairs hallway, I find myself taking my cell phone from my pocket. The intense guilt of a liar creeps over me. Slowly, I press the buttons.

Tides of static wash into my ear. I hear ringing.

Hello?

Hey. It's me.

Mm. Jon? Hello?

Yeah, it's me. Can you hear me?

Um. Sorry, I'm still asleep. Why are you calling me?

I just wanted to talk to you.

Oh. Ouch.

What?

Stubbed my toe. Had to find my watch in the dark. Um. (She sounds annoyed.) So, uh, how is the beach? Are you having *fun*? (Better not be, her tone suggests.)

I didn't have time to go. Unpacking and stuff.

Really. Oh. Well, I'm having a really good time up here.

No, you're not.

You think? Let me ask you something, Jon, can I ask you something?

Okay.

Does it matter to you that you hurt me?

That I hurt you, I repeat.

Jon, I'm sorry I didn't tell you about James. Okay? I'm sorry it didn't end *right that night,* the second I met you, because things can just end instantaneously like that, can't they? You can turn a person off like a faucet. Maybe *you* can do it, but I just don't have the talent. Sorry about that.

She hangs up on me.

I massage my injured hand. James, Ruth, Mursey; a weird jigsaw. I go into my parents' room and lie on their bed. The curtains are closed and the computer is off. It's dark, and I shut my eyes.

* * *

Sometime later I sit up, waking, and stare in the darkness, remembering. Remembering where I am.

I had a dream, or something like a dream. I don't remember what it was, but my stomach is full of moths.

Local News

My parents' computer hums in the darkness. The screen comes on and stains my hands blue, and I search the internet for *Mursey*. Articles begin to appear. There are wire reports with terse sentences.

> Fri May 4, 9:43 PM ET
> *by LISA BOYLE, Associated Press Writer*
>
> BONDURANT, MD - Two former Bondurant High School football players have come forward to claim they were sexually abused by former teacher and coach George Mursey.
> One of the students is now 21 and the other is 22. Frederick County police spokeswoman Dana Gorey said that in both cases, the alleged abuse took place over a period of . . .
> Larson said that hundreds of videotapes and photographs were found in the Mursey home. He said many were filmed in Mursey's home and appear to show an unidentified man crushing small animals, but he would not say whether

I try to read them all the way through, but it's like my eyes *won't*. They try to stick to the page but after a moment, something won't focus.

> Sat May 4, 10: 15 PM ET
> BONDURANT, MD (Reuters) - A third

FIRES

> student from Bondurant High School came forward today to claim that he was sexually abused by his former football coach.
>
> The 16-year-old student said that coach George Mursey had befriended him and

And there are longer articles from local papers—the more local, the longer. Some kind of pride behind the horror.

> Chief Raynard also told local reporters yesterday that FBI officials told him they were looking into the possibility that Mursey kidnapped the boy in another state. The case has garnered national attention for the unusual nature of the crime.
>
> Mursey's ex-wife Diane Leeds, who divorced him in 1989 and now lives in Washington state with their son, told reporters in a short statement Wednesday that she had not seen her ex-husband in ten years.
>
> Raynard described the basement room as having "a terrible smell." He said the upstairs of the house appeared normal, and that Mursey had a large collection of sports memorabilia, including a football signed by the 1991 Washington Redskins. Also a hunting enthusiast, Mursey had stuffed a

And there are awkward editorials from the Bondurant *Gazette*.

> What can we say when something this bad happens in our own neighborhood? There is not much to say. All we can do is take comfort in the fact that we know our neighbors and that our lives are, for the most part, filled with good things. We can also pray, and we can be glad that a child who suffered will now be in peace.
>
> It is important to remember when we find out something bad about someone we trusted that, in fact, most people really are what they seem to be. A good neighbor is a good neighbor. Suspicion is a dangerous thing that can deplete a community if there is too much of it. Of course we should always be careful, but we should also remember the goodness in the people around us.

A soft dying sound comes out of the computer as I shut it down. The shadows of my parents' bedroom huddle around me. I rise and walk to the window, rubbing my hand.

I look into the distance, beyond the Mursey house. I can see the burning mountain. An absolute *wall* of smoke is pouring up, red-stained. I open the window, feel the hot breeze.

sleep

DOWNSTAIRS AGAIN, in the living room, I stare out the glass doors. Far away I see lit houses. A plane crosses the sky.

I lie on the sofa, shoes gone, flexing my bare feet. From across the house I hear, every now and then, the meager noise of a bottle clicking against a glass.

Darkness nuzzles. I'm having half-dreams about Ruth. She's pulling my ribcage apart. She's excavating. *It's okay,* she keeps saying, *it'll be over in a minute.*
I hear footsteps in the hall, then in the kitchen. The fridge opens. Water gurgles. Now footsteps move back down the hall. The front door opens.
And closes.
I used to wander out there sometimes.

* * *

When the waves crest I see gray ice in them. The sky is a glacial, frostbite gray. The beach is ice-crusted.
A seagull with no feathers hops across broken shells. It is pink, like a chicken, and it regards me with stupid black eyes. Freeze-burned skin peels from its body in strips. The bird speaks to me. It has a creaky, childlike voice, and says, *Jon, the people you eat . . . are the regrets that you shit.*
The bird is nonsensical in its delirium. It is euphoric in its suffering.

* * *

I spasm awake. He's sleeping on the floor, his body molded into the angle where the floor meets the wall, and he's babbling in a strange, stripped-away voice.
Let me in, he says. Let me in, let me back in.

ANTOSCA

Bad Morning

SHARP LITTLE CLICKS COME FROM THE KITCHEN. I lift my face, blinking. Sunlight streams through the glass doors, dripping over everything, sticky and gold. It must be about noon.

The sun feels good on my bare arms when I get up, but my wrist is swollen and my knuckles are ringed by violet bruises.

I hear a raw, nasal ripping. Followed by violent hacking—throat-clearing. More sharp clicks, then another raw phlegmy gasp. I recognize the noise at once.

I smell a thousand half-smoked cigarettes when I enter the hall. Through the kitchen arch, he's visible, hunched with love over the counter.

James.

He moves not an inch, giving no indication that he hears. Sinewy muscles are tense under his shirt. Abruptly he straightens, still not looking back.

What is that? Coke? Speed?

James doesn't answer.

What is it? I repeat.

It never occurred to me until now, he says, but where's the dog? Did he take it with him? If he disappeared, he either took it with him or—I don't know what. Let it loose? Listen, if you see that goddamn Dalmatian out there, you let me know, because I'll kill it.

His voice is too fast—not only is it fast, it's trembling a little, like a train shaking on the rails as it accelerates.

What are you talking about—are you okay? Have you slept at all? I slept like a *lamb*.

With that, he pushes past me down the hall, to disappear into the dining room. On the kitchen counter, a pile of dead cigarettes rises like a tumor up from a soup bowl. Did he brings *cartons* with him?

FIRES

Beside the bowl lies his Yale ID, which was making the clicking noises on the counter. In his picture he is smiling. I recognize the photo from the high school yearbook, which means it was taken at the beginning of senior year.

A few inches from the ID are a tiny plastic bag, blue-tinted, and a piece of drinking straw. I can't be certain what was in the bag because he tore it apart and it looks like he licked the inside out. So probably coke.

With the sun glowing in, I stand there. Outside the window, a helicopter circles to drop water on the mountain, and something unpleasant squirms in my chest, like a fetus being strangled.

Wet snuffling sounds come from the other room. I join him there. His nose is weeping. He stares through a gap in the curtains. More police cars are parked across the street.

In the windows of Mursey's house, figures walk back and forth. James sniffles, eyes fixed to the coach's house. Small, arrhythmic noises drag themselves up his throat.

Smoke fills the sky, and ashes darken the air, blowing over the neighborhood. The trees in the front yard rustle and beads of water flicker as the sprinkler distributes them in a gentle circle. The smoke billows, writhing and squirming in the sky. By now the fire must be approaching the far edge of the cornfield.

shower

UNDRESSED IN THE UPSTAIRS BATHROOM, I press my head against the mirror. I cannot get enough air in my lungs.

Gradually, I gather my senses. Footsteps pace downstairs.

Starting the shower, I step under cold, thundering water and lean against the tiles. Yesterday's sweat has gone sour on my skin. Scrubbing it off, I shut my eyes, feel the water raise goose bumps. Behind my eyelids, nightmarish shapes blossom, undersea flowers in fast motion. I have to think. I have to think about what I'm going to do.

I think about walking out this afternoon, back to the train station. When I spit between my feet, I see pink blood against the porcelain. Too many cigarettes. Cold water slaps my skin. I wash listlessly.

There's a soft click. Hands soapy, I freeze. Quiet, unsettling movements are audible. The bathroom door closes.

James?

No answer. Something creaks. Then a sigh.

James? That you?

Water drips in my eyes, burns them.

James, man—you there? What are you doing?

I slip a finger between the shower curtains, discreetly parting them. The sink edge is visible; so are blue-and-white tiles. I push the curtain aside a centimeter and see his shoes, the cuffs of his jeans. He's sitting on the wicker hamper.

That thing'll collapse if you sit on it, I say.

He ignores me. I let the curtain close, hurriedly rinsing soap from my arms. I hear a cigarette lighter scrape. A ghost of smoke exhaled. And he says—

I had nightmares all night, man. I can't—I can't think.

I pause. I watch a clear ripe jewel quiver on the lip of the shower head. His voice is strange. It trembles.

Do you have nightmares?

Uh, sometimes. Are you all right?

No, he says. I'm not joking, man. I'm really, really *not* all right.

A soft impulse fills me and although it's too slippery to get hold of, to hold down and look at, I'm remembering with a poignant and almost visceral throb how much I once wanted his friendship.

I want to ask you something, man, he says.

Yeah, anything.
And be honest. Be fucking honest.
Of course.
He never did *anything* to you, Danfield? Mursey? I mean, he never—?
No.
Silence follows—except the thundering shower—and I blink water out of my eyes. My hair is plastered to my skull and I have goose bumps. I hear him sniffling. Whatever he snorted is dripping down the back of his throat. I want to give him a glass of water to wash it away; I want to make him stop moving, gather the pieces of his personality; I want to help.
It's been a while since I talked to Ruth, he says. It's been too long. Have you talked to her since we got here?
Yeah, actually.
I thought you did. Did you tell her I'm with you?
No.
Good. Good. Hey, you know, I always thought it's kind of strange, man, that the two of you got together. I wouldn't think you'd be her type.
Well, I don't think it's strange. There's nothing strange about it. You know, she doesn't go for guys who aren't kind of fucked up.
Well, I'm all good, man.
There is silence. It is a long, arduous silence during which the water beats against me and my heart beats sickly in my chest.
You want to tell me, I ask carefully, what happened to you at his house?
There is another silence, a perilous one, before he says, All right. All right—I was tortured, and I liked it. Do you believe that?
If you say so.
Tell me the truth, James demands. I mean, come on, you lived

right here. He saw you every *day*. He must have come after you. Sometime. At least once.

No.

A note of disbelief, of pleading, comes into his voice.

Coach Mursey did stuff to the kids from this neighborhood for *years*, he says. Lots of kids I know. And me. How come not you? He saw you every fucking day. How come not *you*?

My skin is cold. I turn the hot water up.

I don't know, I say deliberately. I guess things just work out certain ways.

Why not *you*, he repeats.

The water has turned burning hot.

He sighs. Then he says, Well, I guess I was wrong. I found out you were with Ruth and I thought maybe . . . (He hacks and sniffles; the coke is trickling again.) But I guess not. You know, man, you got lucky. You know what the American dream is? Good parents, a nice neighborhood, college, love, and never having to throw up Vaseline.

You know, I don't know what's real and what's nightmares I had later. But why did I keep going back? What the fuck is wrong with me? Why did I do that?

James pauses, tapping his hand against something. But you know, he says, sometimes people like to pretend bad things that happened to them didn't really happen. I was like that for a while. Telling myself it didn't happen.

There is silence.

I close my eyes and see fireworks by Dali, the world sketched in strange, painful colors. Steam scours my throat. I turn the hot water down.

James sighs, his bait not taken.

I've been out walking, he says. My phlegm's gray from the ash. I broke into the Sheltons' house. It felt good to sit in their chairs, lie in their beds. Then I broke into the Daltons', too. And some others. And then my own house.

Great, I say. That was a really smart idea, breaking into places. When the fire comes, it's not gonna matter.

If. *If* it comes. If not, you may have some explaining to do.

You know, he says, sometimes *people* catch on fire. They burn so hot their bones turn to ash. No shit, I read up on it. You would not believe the combustibility of a human being.

I believe it, James.

The water turns cold. I remain quiet, expecting him to say something else. He doesn't. Instead, I hear him get up to leave.

Drained and sad, I slump against the tiled wall—and then the shower curtain is yanked aside.

The edges of his nose are crusted with blood and his face is childish, afraid, apologetic. Terror leaps up in me—the inexplicable, recoiling terror I felt last night when a black dog went past the window with a shoe in its jaws. I look at his eyes, black-brown and wet, and can't speak. He's two feet from me and water is trickling down my stomach, dripping off my dick.

I just wanted to say, he says slowly, I know maybe it was a mistake to bring you into this. Maybe it's not a thing I had any right to force you into.

He starts to close the curtain, then remembers something.

And I apologize, he tells me, for the fact that you have to deal with me.

He closes the curtain.

Listless

I LOCK THE DOOR. The water dripping down my body makes me

think of saliva and tongues. I don't have an erection, but my adrenaline is pumping so hard I feel like I'm riding two hits of ecstasy, and I want, need, *must have* sex.

Leaning against the wall I masturbate with my uninjured hand, now deliberately thinking of nothing but my own cock, and then I come, cough, dry heave, and start to cry.

Finally I wipe my face and dry off, shaking, and spit blood-ribboned saliva in the toilet. It floats there, a limp jellyfish, and I press my knuckles against my eyelids. Sunbursts. Downstairs, I hear him pacing. I open my eyes. His extinguished cigarette lies curled in the sink. I drop it in the trash. In the mirror I'm growing a sketchy beard.

To waste time, I shave. A stippled mess of facial hair ends up in the sink along with a single drop of blood. The pain feels good and necessary, so I shave again pointlessly, drawing tiny beads of blood, and breathe, and sigh.

In the back of my throat I'm tasting god knows what.

Dressed, I go into my parents' bedroom. I go to the window. Detectives stand on Mursey's lawn, conferring, sweat stains on their armpits. The sky is a wall of white smoke and swirling ashes and it towers over the nervous little batch of cops like a pillar of heaven.

The cops are craning to look at something. Pointing. I lean carefully forward, looking down the street.

White-tailed deer. Maybe eight or ten, thin-legged and graceful, crossing the street on slender, precarious legs. Muscles flowing like hot liquid under their hides. One stops to lick a mailbox. A few deer stop to look around, their black eyes blinking intelligently, and then they continue on, crossing a driveway, trampling a flower garden, pausing to taste a boxwood bush.

They pass between two houses and are gone. A migration. But

they are just going toward the access road, which will lead them to the McDonald's and the Park-n-Ride, and other things like that.

When I go downstairs, James is gone. I feel relief, then anger that he went off somewhere without me. It's stupid with those cops out there. But I can't shake a feeling of abandonment. Like overtaxed piano wires, my nerves are playing sour, unpredictable notes.

I search the fridge. I'm keyed-up, nervous. The desire for sex has become a desire for food—I haven't eaten anything since the chicken wings and steamed vegetables, eighteen hours ago. I take out rye bread, provolone, and mayonnaise. There's bacon in the freezer so I chip off five strips and put them in the microwave.

While they're sputtering I go in the living room to watch the news. CNN says a smoke jumper is dead.

Back in the kitchen, I spread mayonnaise on rye and lay slices of American cheese on it. The microwave is dripping with hot, exploded grease. After I dry the bacon on a paper towel, I make a sandwich, slice it in half.

I pour a glass of orange juice. A bottle of cooking sherry sits by the stove and I add some to the juice. It tastes like a fermented screwdriver—awful.

The clock says two in the afternoon—where the fuck is James? My loneliness is a languid, queasy force that seems to limit my physical movements. I half-listen to the news as I eat, licking bacon grease and mayo from my fingers. *Governor Conlon visited the Alleghenies yesterday afternoon, pledging resources to fight the blaze, which ranks as the largest forest fire in the history of the eastern United States... said that bureaucratic unpreparedness and miscommunication between the NIFC and local fire authorities led to repeated delays...* I begin wolfing down the second half of the sandwich. *Authorities cautioned that heavy, shifting winds which are expected Monday afternoon could...*

Finished the sandwich, I rip open a bag of potato chips and eat them in handfuls, listening. *In other news* . . . I pour more sherry into my empty glass, not bothering with orange juice. . . . *no new leads about Mursey's whereabouts* . . .

I dash into the living room. A file photo of Coach Mursey is displayed on the screen, but the image is already changing to a story about an Amtrak derailment.

I go back upstairs and stare out the picture window. There's a new mountain and it is ash-white, churning.

In my pocket, the phone vibrates.

Fuck, I whisper.

I answer, but the connection breaks. CALL ENDED 00:09.

I check the RECEIVED CALLS log, wincing as I press buttons with my injured hand, but the fucking phone hasn't recorded it. I understand that. Because somewhere along the way I slipped into a world that looks real—except for the colossal, nightmarish fire about to destroy the history of my life. This isn't the real world, and things don't have to make sense.

Again the phone vibrates.

Hello?

Jon?

I can't hear you . . .

It's *me*. Ruth.

Hey. How are you?

She laughs bitterly and the static is like thistles on her voice. Sorry I sort of hung up on you last time.

It's okay. I can't talk long, okay?

Oh. Okay. So—is it sunny? The beach? Is it like before?

It's beautiful. The waves are warm.

Can I be honest with you, Jon? I miss you. And I don't understand you.

FIRES

Ruth . . .

What?

Nothing. Never mind.

I watch a helicopter swerve through the billowing smoke.

I gotta go.

Already?

Yeah. Look, I've—I've gotta go. The connection's about to cut out, anyway. And I gotta help my grandma.

She's there?

Yeah, she's—in the other room. And I gotta help her make dinner.

Doesn't the nurse guy do it?

Not tonight.

Oh. Well, tell her I said hi. Did she ask about me?

Yeah, she did.

After the call, I stare out the window. Smoke owns the sky. Detectives are coming out of Coach Mursey's house, carrying boxes, sweat glistening on their foreheads. I close the blinds.

I lie down on my parents' bed. The clock says it's close to three in the afternoon. Pale shadows on the ceiling. I do not move. I wonder where James is. I remember lying on the beach with Ruth, and I remember feeling as if my blood were not blood but something else, something alcoholic. I grope for that feeling. There's nothing.

A dream unfolds slowly. I am outdoors. Ashes float in the air. I follow a herd of deer, watching tendons ripple in their flanks, watching their long muscular necks duck to avoid branches. Sometimes they look back at me with their large black eyes. The air feels cool, and the swirling of the smoke and ash in the sky is peaceful, like a summer storm gathering in plum-purple clouds, a great sad bruise. Something is coming for me, is coming *back* for me.

The deer glide across lawns, along the edges of swimming pools, across asphalt roads. They have brown freckles. They are fleeing to a mountain just a mile or so to the east . . . its silhouette is a blue-green that melts into dusk. This mountain does not exist in real life.

* * *

Darkness lashes down like a storm over my dreams, convulsive, quivering darkness, and a face flickers in the darkness—Ruth's face—and she's afraid of me because I've begun to shed my skin in great sloughing heaps, but I can't understand what's happening.

The Houses

WHAT WAKES ME IS THE TERRIBLE SILENCE. Through the open door I should be able to hear the whole house; I hear nothing. When I roll over to look at the alarm clock, it's blank.

Rising, I find myself afraid; this kind of silence has no place in suburbia. Where is the arid hum of the fridge? The soft dry rattle of ceiling fans? The whisper of central air? I am on edge.

Filled with half-awake dread, I go downstairs. Alone, into the living room. The mid-afternoon shadows are long and muted and they feel like threats.

I am drawn by something dark and jealous and sexual to the glass doors. A tiny, blue-tinted plastic bag lies on the coffee table. It has been licked clean.

The swelling of my hand is worse. The wrist won't bend anymore. I look out through the doors on a neighborhood that is quiet as a sacrificial lamb.

It's benign, yeah.
He's out there.
It's a human sacrifice, that's what it is.

FIRES

The glass doors whisper as I slide them open. And I step out onto the patio, into the air which is an unholy blend of perfume—grass clippings, gasoline—and the incense of hell, the burning mountain. Mid-afternoon that feels like dusk.

Going down the wood stairs, I get momentary, vertiginous déjà vu: I am going into my backyard to mow the lawn, because Dad told me to, and I'm going to do it fast, because after this I can go over to Sara's before her parents get home and we'll lie on her bed with its neatly arranged stuffed animals and maybe she'll let me take her shirt off. An erection presses against my pants. The sky is blue.

Then all that is gone, and I'm back here. Standing behind my house under the gray smoke sky, the hummingbird feeder nearby like a weird antenna. A tomblike shadow blankets the land. This is a strange, dark doppelganger of my neighborhood.

I scan the backyards, scan the maple trees and swimming pools, the flower gardens and barbecue grills. I cough up dark phlegm and deposit it in the dirt, then raise my face again and walk toward the far end of the yard.

Looking out across the panorama of lawns and John Deere mowers and empty patios, I begin to feel obscurely thrilled, and I remember wanting, as we stood outside James's house last night, to go inside. I feel that again, amplified, for every house I see. These are museums of the America I live in, and prurient, guilty desire seizes me: I want to explore.

I go over the back fence into the Jensens' backyard. Before I've taken five steps, I see James's path: the Jensens' patio doors are smashed. And when I go up on their patio, I tread carefully to avoid all the broken shards of glass.

On the patio there's a picnic table and a green-striped umbrella. There are dead potted plants and an empty watering can. There is a child's teddy bear that's been sitting out. It looks crisp. Dirty shoes. A barbecue grill.

Oddly jittery, I take a deep breath, then I step inside the Jensen house, and it feels like one of those dreams where you're wandering for no reason except that this is the dream where you wander. You're in a kind of fugue state. Nothing matters, since no one's around to stop you.

The Jensen house is dark, like ours. Something occurs to me, and I lift the receiver of their telephone and listen: no dial tone. I wonder how long it's been out. It doesn't matter, though—I have my cell phone.

As I wander the house, I see artifacts and touch them. I open the fridge and touch Tropicana orange juice, Peter Pan peanut butter, Hunt's ketchup. I touch small glass figurines of cats. I touch the smashed face of the TV. I touch the ripped-out pages of a child's book that are scattered around the carpet like leaves. I touch the stuffing James ripped out of the loveseat.

When I walk out the Jensens' front door, rubbing my aching hand, the world still looks dreamlike. The afternoon sky is billowy, dusky, and although the fire is behind me, I can smell it and distantly hear it.

There are no people in sight, no human sounds, and my disconnection from other human beings chokes me. But James is here somewhere, very close. Probably in one of the houses I can see from where I'm standing. Yet everything seems deserted, and like a sleepwalker I drift across the Jensens' lawn.

It doesn't take long to find the next house he's been to. I go in through a broken picture window. There's glass everywhere. I call his name. The damage here is worse. I walk around surveying the wreckage, touching a VCR into whose black mouth old macaroni and cheese has been packed. I see a heap of Fresh Step cat litter which appears to have been set on fire. I see a miserable-looking houseplant with thick leaves which have been partially eaten.

In the next hours, I visit the Foltzes', the Carmichaels', the Ellisons', the Wechslers', and the Kipen-Shapiros'. I see thousands of dollars worth of damage but no James. Yet he's here, in a way; I can almost smell his rage—and his piss, on the Ellisons' sofa—lingering in the air behind him, like the scent of an animal marking its territory. But what unnerves me most in all these homes is their similarity to my house, and to that house across the street from mine—Mursey's.

I avoid the basements. And as I'm walking back home, across the solemn dry lawns, across asphalt streets, past boxwood shrubs and dying azaleas, I feel defeated, unsatisfied, not just because I didn't find James but because none of those houses were *the* house, the one that has grown to assume a totemic significance in my mind.

He is not back at the house. It is almost dusk, and as I stand at the dining room window, I can see the police gearing up to leave. The fire is close. If it hasn't reached the cornfield yet, it will have by tonight or tomorrow morning.

I feel like I'm expiring, winding down.

Upstairs, back in my parents' room, I lie on the bed.

Honey-colored light stains the blinds, the color of a red sun beginning to set, filtered through smoke. The light starts to turn orange, and I lie in bed watching it rust.

Around me the house is silent. My nerves settle a little, but my senses are acute. The air is watercolor blue, muddy with strange shadows. I have the sense of things slowly beginning to happen, quiet gears turning in the world.

I listen.

And I can hear it. In the distance—a low roar like a train. I feel it in my guts. It's coming for us, coming to burn down our trees and eat our neighborhood.

I lift my head. He's in the doorway, in the shadows. His eyes and

mouth are smudges. Neither of us says anything. Not for a while. When he does speak, it is just to say one thing:
The cops are gone.

Across the Street

I GET UP FROM THE BED.
I follow him downstairs.
He smells like wine and ten thousand cigarettes. In the darkness, I hear muffled gunshots: his knuckles cracking. Blue-black shadows hang from the walls. Nothing breathes, nothing speaks.
In the dining room he pours himself a glass of wine. I stare out into the beginnings of twilight. The police cars are gone. He sips his wine. His blond hair is dusty and dirty; his face has fresh scratches on it. Then again, so does mine—the razor blade. My heart is stammering. Dusk light stains the curtains.
Let's go, he says quietly. Only now, as he lowers his glass and we go into the hall, do I notice the trembling in his hands.
We step outside into livid twilight. A pillar of smoke hides the dying sun, but rose-wine light spills over the neighborhood.
A warm breeze brings ash, throws it in our eyes, our mouths, and it tastes like nothing I know. Like disintegrated leaves, maybe, or dead moths. The whole neighborhood is suspended in heavy amber light and no birds cross the sky.
We cross the lawn.
James walks onto the edge of Mursey's grass, which needs mowing. I follow him, breathing ashes. Did I grow up here?
We approach the porch. Mursey's yard is empty, with no trees or bushes to obscure the house, which is friendly and visible like the face of an old friend.

FIRES

It has a clumsy, sated look, like a cat that has eaten many birds.

On the porch there's the empty wicker chair where Mursey used to sit, his dog beside him, and the white table where he would set his coffee.

James picks up a smooth rock from the flower garden. He mounts the steps and shatters the glazed glass beside the door, then reaches in, gropes, and unlocks it. I wonder about the alarm system, but nothing seems to happen.

I climb the porch stairs with bad air in my lungs. Police tape is stretched over the door. But it opens inward, revealing darkness.

We duck under the tape and go in.

A mirror hangs politely just inside the door. Reflected in it, two strangers. I sense something in the air—the presence of a secret history skinning layers of time and identity off me.

There's electricity, something, going through me. Something I didn't expect, like a white-hot hand moving around inside me. Something in me recoils into itself.

I force myself forward.

The house, in its briny shadows, is like all others. Like my house. In the decisive silence, I see the same hallway, the same rooms.

It is a fine house.

Everything is up to snuff. Nothing is disorderly. The person who lived in this house had self-control, had discipline, had the will to keep a clean home.

There are blank spaces on the living room floor, indicating items removed by the police. James drifts ahead, looking humbled by ferocious awe. He's trembling a little and staring at things—a baseball bat on the mantle, a small volume of Billy Collins poetry, a cracked vase.

ANTOSCA

The kingly head and neck of male deer are mounted above the fireplace. Its antlers, spread like eagle wings, are the color of smokers' teeth. Seizing the antlers, James rips the thing down from the wall, sends it crashing to the floor. He kneels over it and with his pocketknife he stabs the back of the deer's neck and begins sawing a hole there. When the hole is big enough, he plunges his hand in, rips out handfuls of sawdust and stuffing. Then he's got something else, a white envelope. He opens it—film negatives spill out. Then they're gone, in his pocket, and he's standing up again.

I'll burn these, he says.

That's what you came here to get? I say.

I'll burn them.

Knowing better than to ask what they show, I back away, massaging my wrist, looking at things other than James, and I wonder out loud if we'll go up to the second floor. But James looks at me with a kind of recoiling irritation that says: *One step at a time, all right?*

Let's go downstairs first, he says.

The basement door is in the kitchen, beside the pantry. We find ourselves pulled toward it. Quiet, unsure. Gray light, with a wisp of gold, filters in the kitchen window. The basement door is closed.

I say, Well, I'm ready if you are.

James opens the door. We descend.

We enter a darkness of a different kind. It is tropical and stagnant, and our shoes on the concrete frighten up dust in pale, fussy flowers. The air has something horrible in it.

A cigarette lighter gnashes its teeth, and the sudden, trembling flame throws a crematorium glow on James's lower jaw as he lights another cigarette—and for just a moment I see his black-brown eyes in the glow, then the flame goes out, and nothing is visible but the eye of his cigarette. It moves away from me.

There's a scraping, the sound of dry paint cracking, then gray light enters the basement on a gust of warm—but fresh—air that smells of ashes. The windows, James says, they were painted over.

Dry grass and the rear wheels of a lawnmower—the one I used to use, years ago—are visible in the open window. Far-off human voices are audible, ragged and frantic below the godlike roar-whisper of the fire.

They're at the cornfield, James whispers, listening. He looks around.

Gray light reveals the basement. Dirty tool shelves, benches, Black & Decker drills. A ratty loveseat, half-reupholstered, with stuffing bulging from the side like entrails. A length of coiled chain. Dutch Boy paint. A baby chainsaw. Cans of soup—*hundreds* of them, as if we're in a bomb shelter.

And one more thing, although we don't notice at first. A door.

Except the door is weirdly small, barely three feet high, like a magic door through which a girl might pursue a troll in a fairy tale. You'd have to be on hands and knees. The door has a silver handle and three exterior locks, as well as a slot for passing things through. Great oak shelves, loaded with power tools and cinderblocks, are propped against the walls beside it.

Is that it? I ask. Is it behind that wall?

He doesn't answer. Dust infiltrates my nostrils, makes me hack. The air smells like apple wood, barbecued. He extinguishes his cigarette slowly beneath his shoe, leaving a black mark on the concrete.

Let's go in, he whispers.

Neither of us moves. We stare at the silver handle, the three locks.

You ever been down here before? I ask. Down in the basement?

Yeah.

Have you ever been—in there?

No.

ANTOSCA

Did you have any idea?

I'm honestly not sure if I did or not.

Still neither of us goes forward. The light is turning the color of warm tea.

I'm going in now, he says with sudden, horrible detachment.

He kneels on the dirty floor, puts his hand on the knob, turns it. The three locks are unbolted. He eases the door open. Darkness waits beyond it. And he crawls into it, swallowed quietly.

James? James?

Yeah.

What's in there?

It's a room. A long room.

A 'long room'?

Kind of like a hallway.

To where?

Nowhere, you fucking idiot.

I want to come in and see.

So come.

I hug the concrete and crawl in after him.

The air smells like old blood and shit. Almost no light enters with me; I sense space, open darkness, extending to my left and right. I flick my cigarette lighter, and in its light, I see the bizarre room. It's long, forty feet end to end. It must span almost an entire side of the house, but in width it is less than four feet. It is, exactly as James described, a hallway to nowhere.

I can stand up, though; the ceiling is normal height. The room is empty; if there was anything here, the police took it. Greasy stains, like birthmarks, darken the walls. As do brown bloodstains. The slaughterhouse-outhouse smell is faint but nauseating. On the floor is a chalk outline, so thin, of a very insubstantial person.

FIRES

When the lighter burns my thumb, I let the flame go out. My throat's clogged with phlegm and ash. The stench is nudging me toward a dry heave.

James edges past me in the close darkness. His footsteps move down the room and stop.

When I flick the lighter again, he's sitting on the concrete with darkness around him in curtains. He sits, palms pressed to the floor, the smell of burning forests blending with the odors of shit and suffering. Again the lighter burns my thumb; again I let the flame die.

You know something? he says when it is dark.

What?

I don't remember much of what happened to me in this house.

Oh.

Yeah, it's just a sort of fog covering everything, I can see some of it but it's blurry, like my vision went bad. I think my brain just refuses to remember, you know, from upstairs. And I also think he gave me a few drugs. I mean, I would drink tea or coffee that he would give me, or liquor, and I think he put some stuff in that. Things are grey. I think maybe for some of the other people the drugs had a stronger effect and they can't even remember as much as I can, but I was—you know, I was strong. I mean, I was in really good shape. I don't think he quite dosed me enough.

It smells so bad down here, I say.

I said I would tell you what happened to me upstairs. What happened to me was that I started having a, you know, a relationship with a person, a man. It's just that this man, this person, he was— well, how to say this? You think you know someone and you're going down this road with them, one step at a time, sort of looking at your feet and not seeing where the road is going.

The air doesn't circulate down here at all, I say, feeling lightheaded suddenly.

ANTOSCA

After a certain point I don't remember things, he says. There's a blank, a week or so is blank. Want to know one thing I do remember? Very clearly?

You do remember something, I say.

Right at the beginning of it, as it was just sort of started but it hadn't gotten into what it would become yet, he was driving me home one night or something. Yeah, from a practice, I think. We're on the road and we're laughing and stuff, because we always really got along, it was like hanging out with an uncle, or something, somebody who had authority and you could trust but wasn't *an authority*, like your dad or, well, your coach.

Yeah, okay, I say.

So we stop at a light, it's dark, it's night, and in the headlights we see the light shining back in something's eyes, very close to the ground. At first I think it's a fox but then it sort of slinks out of a bush and you can see it's a sort of reddish cat, like a very well-cared-for one, probably an expensive one. And Mursey says, 'That's somebody's cat.' He stops the car, gets out very carefully, and walks toward it. You'd expect it to just dash away, but he approaches *very* carefully, *very* slowly, kind of gently coaxing it over. He licks his hands for it to smell, so it's curious, and finally he just scoops it up, quick and gentle. When he brings it back to the car, it's totally purring. Some cats will go nuts in a car but this one just sits there the whole ride home, purring like crazy. We get home and he brings the cat inside, lets it meet his Dalmatian, makes sure they'll play nice. He says, 'I'm keeping this cat. I think we're gonna be friends.'

He had a cat? I say. I don't remember ever seeing a cat.

Yeah, well. Anyway, then he and I sit and have a beer and that's when things really go dark. For the next five or six weeks, things go dark a lot. The thing is, it's all very confusing. I can't even remember for sure how I *felt*. I know I wasn't feeling good, or calm—but

FIRES

I didn't *hate* him. I kept going to his house. And when it ended, it wasn't because I, like, broke free or something. I think he just got bored. Us, the guys from the neighborhood, I guess he was just playing with us. And I remember that I didn't feel relieved, I felt hurt, and then I felt angry. That was the first time I stood up to him, can you believe that, I fought back because he said I had to *stop* coming over. I wanted to hurt him, so I said, 'I've got this on you, now, what if I start talking about it? They'll come for you, you know that.' At first he's talking all calm, doesn't seem perturbed, like kids have threatened him with this before, and he's saying, 'You wouldn't do that, we're friends, we're friends,' like that. Sort of casually making coffee while this is going on, and the red cat is walking across the table, and he stops to pet it, real calm.

Didn't he have, like, pictures of you, also? I ask, very carefully. James ignores this.

But I won't shut up, I'm like, 'I have this on you forever, you know that? So what do I get out of it, what are you going to do for me, to keep me happy?' Then suddenly he turns and me and says, 'What is wrong with you? Do you *not think* I can make you hurt?' Then he grabs the cat by its neck, picks it up all fighting and clawing, and throws it in the oven. Turns the oven on. I sort of take a half-step toward the oven and he's just *on* me, knocks me to the linoleum face-down and is talking in this regular voice while kneeling on top of me, not straddling me but with his actual knees on my back, all two hundred fifty pounds of him, and saying, 'What is wrong with you? Do you *not* think I will go to your house? Do you *not* think I will do to them, your mother and father, what I did to you, and let you watch?' And all the time I can hear the cat screaming in the oven, and finally stop screaming.

You do remember something, I say.

Yes, Jon—yes, I remember that.

ANTOSCA

You thought he found someone else, I say lightheadedly. Someone from the neighborhood, from around here. To replace you.

Yes, he said. That's what I thought.

I say nothing. My eyes have adjusted, but the faint, persistent smell of pain and blood and excrement still makes me want to be sick. I breathe only when necessary.

I think, My adolescence took place just across the street. My room was the center of the world. And it was a healthy and normal world with long friendly tendrils that extended into town and from there out into the universe. Families, lovers, children, pets.

Again I flick my lighter to see James, and part of me wants to offer some kind of sympathy—but another part flinches from the idea, as if he's diseased and I shouldn't go near.

Are you going anywhere else? I ask. Upstairs?

No. *No.*

Suddenly a dry-heave doubles me over.

I'll be back, I gasp. In a minute. Back in a minute.

I get on my knees, pressed to the filthy concrete, and crawl out. The light in the basement has gone husky blue, and the raw smell of heat and ashes is almost refreshing. I suck air into my lungs as I stagger up the basement stairs.

Night is near, the kitchen is darker. I go into the hallway, to the stairs.

I take a step up the stairs, and then something happens in my stomach, I don't know what. And I don't want to go up any further. I *could*—it's not like I *can't*—but I just really don't want to. I really don't want to.

So I take a step back down, and then I'm not on the stairs anymore.

Suppressing another dry heave—it's still in my lungs, the shit and blood—I walk to the rear of the house. I stand at the glass patio

FIRES

doors—police tape stretched across them—and look outside. Not far off, beyond a row of rooftops, the fire crawls onward. A light wind makes the black shapes of maples rustle and shiver. The fire has not yet reached the cornfield.

But it's close, so close. And after the cornfield, the neighborhood. A tinderbox of histories. What did they cost?

I think of virgins and calves. That kind of sacrifice has a place in human history, I think, but sometimes it isn't called by its name. Or it happens in secret. Perhaps lives like mine exist, I think, not in spite of, but because of, the secret histories that lope along beside them.

Figures are moving in the distance. Firefighters. What are they doing? They've surrounded a house that is not on fire and they're hosing it down with water.

I'm slumping in Mursey's kitchen, lighting a cigarette. I rest there and smoke. I stare at the microwave, the cabinets, the empty sink. Everything looks so familiar, so familiar. Then I go back down the basement stairs.

Night has descended fully, and without the lighter it's too dark to see. In the glow, I look around. The little door is closed.

James? I say.

I kneel, the metal band of the lighter growing hot against my thumb, and for an instant I imagine him trapped behind that door. And when I open it he'll be blind, with blue-white skin, smelling of shit and death. He may beg. Or perhaps he'll be silent, having learned the vanity of begging. I've lived here for years. This is my house. This is my life. I teach school, I drive a Saturn, I have a prisoner.

My head twitches, quick, as if shaking off invisible gnats. I open the door and crawl in. The stench. I glimpse James, sitting on the dirty floor with his head lowered.

Then my thumb burns, and I let the flame go out. But there's nothing to see, really, and nothing to say. And I am utterly tired.

A few moments later, I flick the lighter one more time and its sulky glow captures him; he's a collage of shadows and rusted, wavery light. Head lowered, eyes hidden.

I'm going home, I say. Coming?

In a while, man.

In Limbo

I STEP OUTSIDE AND SMELL THE WORLD BURNING.

A warm wind blows ashes over the neighborhood and snows them on houses, on swimming pools. Maple trees shiver gently and whisper to each other; I turn and look at the mountain. The wind, with its listless gray snow, is silky on my face.

I feel hollowed out.

I look up at a black and billowing sky where no stars exist and the moon is a flickering crescent behind veils of smoke. From dark streets away, I hear the fire—and human voices, indecipherable, helpless.

I no longer belong here. Within twenty-four hours I'll be gone, and I do not think I'm coming back. Tomorrow, in the afternoon, I'll go to the beach. I'll let the sun bleach out my brain. What I need is to have my whole fucking head destroyed and made again. Obliteration, a stone dagger to the cerebellum.

Things are happening quickly now. Ashes spill through the sky; men scream to each other in the distance.

The shadows of the dining room drape me as I sit at the table, drinking wine, smoking. Nothing moves except the ashes that fall from my cigarette.

FIRES

In the darkness, I rise. With the still-burning cigarette and the half-empty bottle, I go upstairs, into my parents' room, where my cell phone still lies on the bed.

Dialing, I stare out the window into an orange-stained black sky, and soon thorny ringing comes from the phone, from a void.

A fuzzed-out click. Then, from hundreds of miles away:

Hi, you've reached the Zaydmans' . . . we're not here right now, so please leave a message with your name and number, and we'll call you back as soon as we can!

Hi, I say quietly. Ruth, it's Jon. Um, I was just calling to, I don't know, see how you are. I hope you're, um, okay. All right. I'll, I'll call you back.

After a moment, lonely, I go into the hall. The shadows are lugubrious, like syrup. I walk through them and a certain deadness in my soul, a desire to feel something, drives me to the closed door of my bedroom. Behind that door, in poses of unselfconscious earnestness, crouch the tangled emotions of adolescence—the unquenchable lusts, the luridly simplistic convictions. I feel the emptiness in myself where nostalgia should be.

The doorknob is, oddly, cold to the touch. I twist it and the door opens. The darkness within is made of a thicker and more glutinous substance. I flick my cigarette lighter. In the pallid glow, I see my blue carpet, my bed, my desk, my bookshelf, my former life. Heaped in the closet are dust-skinned board games, atlases and encyclopedias, Halloween costumes, wedding suits I grew out of, a fishing rod, a baseball bat, a lava lamp. I feel nothing. Just a faint, incoherent sensation akin to stepping on a dry snakeskin.

I let the flame go out. Darkness closes in. I back out of the room.

I drift into the kitchen, through reefs of shadow, thinking of the tiny dark moles on Ruth's shoulders and at the base of her spine. I

ANTOSCA

feel a desperate, almost panicked desire to get out of this house, this neighborhood. I don't belong here anymore; I did not come from this place. The past lied to me. I need violent, drastic change. But for now, with a feeling of helplessness, I make a sandwich.

The food is warm and tastes bad. Power's been out a long time. I throw the mayonnaise and bacon away, and for my sandwich there's only butter, salt, and a wrinkled tomato. Everything's running out, being finished. I drain a bottle of wine.

The front door slams and I hear his footsteps. His feet pad into the living room.

A moment elapses before I rise, my chair squeaking peevishly on the kitchen tiles. The smell of wood smoke is strong.

In the living room he's shirtless, his long lean body stretched on the sofa.

We have to go in the morning, I tell him quietly. It's close. You got what you came for.

I know.

So you'll come? In the morning?

Of course I'll come.

Good.

He sits up, massaging his face. He looks melted down. Melted down to something dazed, naked, raw.

I'm fucking exhausted, he says. But I know I'm not gonna sleep. At school I used to have these dreams, you know, where I'd come home and find him and kill him. I wonder if I'll ever see him again.

I simply sigh, refusing to acknowledge this. Well, I say, it's better anyway if we don't sleep. Make sure we get out of here early, I mean.

He keeps massaging his face. The scent of his body is an indescribable musk of smoke and staleness.

Don't worry about it, you can sleep. I'll wake you. I'm gonna be up all fucking night. (His face twists up.) *Fuck.* Christ, my head hurts. Christ.

FIRES

Maybe you *should* sleep.

I told you I can't.

He lies back on the sofa, twitching with a kind of restless, hunted tension.

I'll wake you early, he assures me.

You want to go have a smoke outside? I ask.

I'm just going to lie here and think.

Fair enough, then.

Getting up, I return to the kitchen where I light another cigarette and look out the window. The stars are almost invisible.

I watch the red tip of my cigarette glowing. The night creeps by, the fire creeps toward us.

At some point James gets up and goes upstairs. I stare out the window at distant lights, windows of homes that haven't been deserted. Another reality.

I hear him upstairs, going from room to room. Small noises drift down—sounds like he's rummaging through things.

My cigarette is almost out; the filter burns my fingers when I drag. I blow pale smoke at the window. Feet clomp down the stairs. I hear the front door yanked open.

Hey! I call, suddenly alarmed, Where you going? You going back over there?

No, no. Just to my house.

I hear the door close.

Memories come in streaks of hot, melted color.

The vivid blue of swimming pools, a million swimming pools. Wasps, lazy, the color of dark blood. Girls in bathing suits on their towels on the hot concrete. Little kids dashing past. *Don't run by the pool!* Gold-green flies spoiling the food. Dogs pawing the fence, smelling pizza and pretzels with yellow mustard. God, the colors.

ANTOSCA

Sighing, I put my cigarette out in the sink.

James returns after midnight. A warm, smoky wind rushes into the house. I hear him walk to the bathroom. I'm drinking wine in the kitchen. Red wine—I pour it into a dirty glass.

The flush of a toilet, then James's feet go to the living room. Then nothing, silence. Finally his slow feet come down the hall. James appears in the kitchen doorway. I can't tell whether he's looking at me or not. A white plastic mask hides his whole face.

I recognize it. He got it from my bedroom closet, part of an old Halloween costume. A kabuki mask. An impassive, wax-white, androgynous face devoid of emotion or personality. It's made of hard, unbendable, white plastic. The eye holes are dead, black ovals.

Hey, he says, taking off the mask. Look what I found in your room. I'm gonna wear this.

With a movement that's vaguely defiant, he slides the mask back on, hiding his face.

Man, take that thing off. It's creepy.

No.

I shrug, although it *is* creepy. But I simply drink my wine and say nothing, and after a few minutes he disappears.

The earliest hours of morning arrive, bringing a deadness of the soul, a calmness of the flesh. I go into the living room. James isn't there. I curl up on the sofa.

Sleep comes in installments. Bizarre dreams. I squirm around on the cushions, fold myself into a fetal position.

* * *

In the darkness I'm fumbling for the phone.
. . . Hello?

Hey. Did I wake you?
Um. Yeah. But it's okay.
Sorry. You left a message on the machine and you sounded kind of—sad.
Yeah. Just, um, just a few—fuck, I can't think straight. I can barely hear you.
Is everything okay?
Yeah.
You go to the beach today?
Yeah.
I've been watching the news.
Yeah? So have I.
It's almost at your house. Will they be able to stop it?
Fuck, I don't know. (I look around the dark room; I'm alone.) Ruth, that's where I am. I'm here.
I know. There's static but I can hear you barely.
No, Ruth. I'm at home.
You—wait, what?
I came home.
What? Talk loud, okay?
I'm *home*. At my *house*.
What? Yeah, I know. Jon? Are you there?
No, no. I *never went to the beach*, Ruth. Ruth, can you hear me?
You're at *your* house? In Maryland? Isn't it evacuated? Like, where the fire is, you're talking about?
Yes.
Your family's there?
No, they're in New Jersey. They think I'm in Vermont. With you.
You're just at your house by yourself?
I—well, no.
Jon? Who's with you?

Ruth, it's—
Is there someone else? What's going on?
Do you remember James?
(Static crackles.)
Dearborn?
Yes.
(More static. I wait. Finally she speaks again.)
What about James?
He's here with me.
What?
It's—
Wait, wait, Jon—you're with James? Why? (A hint of panic comes into her voice.) Why are you with James?
Ruth, I don't know—it has to do with, with things that happened here. A long time ago.
You didn't try to start anything with him, did you? About him hurting me? I hope not. And don't, Jon, because he'll hurt you. He'll hurt you worse than he means to, even. And he'll *mean* to hurt you.
(But she says this tenderly, almost sorrowfully, as if talking about someone who has cancer. And then there is a pause, in which she presumably tries to puzzle certain things out, tries to absorb all this new information I've thrown at her. When she breaks the static-frosted silence, her voice is quieter and oddly thoughtful.)
You actually knew him well then? she says. Back in high school, you talked to each other?
Kind of, I guess.
So what *happened* back then?
Huh?
To him.
How do you mean?
I mean whatever it was that happened to him. In a house some-

where. He never told me, exactly, but he had nightmares every night, he'd cry about a dog and—

Ruth.

Jon? Hello?

Were you in love with him?

Well . . .

Oh, fucking wonderful.

Jon, don't do this. I love *you* now. Hello?

I'm here.

I love *you*, Jon.

(Silence. I let her suffer. I suffer. I feel the weight of a past that keeps changing shape on me. Finally I speak.)

So what *did* he tell you? What happened to him in that house?

I don't know. I told you. Nothing. He'd say things when he was drunk, details, but never really anything coherent. I thought at first maybe his dad had taken him to some house and molested him, but the more I heard, it didn't seem to make sense. The details never really fit together. There was something about a room, a room up some stairs. Hello? Can you hear me?

What happened there? What'd he say?

I don't know. He would talk about a dog, there was something about a dog. The dog scared him. A black and white dog.

What else?

Nothing else. He got so upset he threw up on me once.

That's it? There's more. There must be. And I want to know about you and him. I want to know everything. Why did you let him hurt you?

What do you want me to say, Jon? He fucked up my life. There's stuff missing in his head. At first it was fascinating, I guess, but then it was scary. And drugs made it worse, much worse. His behavior, everything—he would have breakdowns, basically.

ANTOSCA

He hasn't always been like that. Something made him that way.

I don't know, Jon, I really don't. But *something* happened. You've never seen him naked, have you? He has scars.

Tell me more. I want to know more.

I told you—Hello? The connection—can you hear me? I told you, he never really talked about it unless he was—

No, I want to know about *you and him*.

Suddenly the connection cuts off. Nothing. Furiously, cursing in the darkness, I redial her number. When she picks up, the first thing she says is:

I already fucking told you, Jon. There's nothing more to tell.

What was it like, being with him? Tell me that.

Shit, I don't know. He needed—he—I don't know, he just needed someone. And I tried to be that person. But he's too far gone.

You feel guilty.

Jon, *believe me*, I'm not in love with him anymore. Do you understand? Don't do this. Hello—still there? Listen, be careful, Jon, okay?

Be careful?

Jon, he hates you.

He does?

Well, he still wants *me*, there's no doubt about that. But then again he's not really one for subterfuge, he's not good at it. If he's there with you, he would have hurt you already if that's what he wanted. Maybe he's replacing me with you.

Replacing?

Hello? You still hear me?

Mostly static.

Listen to me, Jon. He's in a hell and he's out to destroy himself. If it's just the two of you there then you have to watch him. Don't let him hurt himself. Do you—

FIRES

Do I? Hello? You're breaking up.
—you.
What? Hello?
—said don't—
Try to . . . ? Hello? Ruth?
. . .
Hello? Hello?

Desperately I attempt to call back again, but there's no reception. EXTENDED NETWORK flashes, but the call won't connect. Minutes later I try again and get the same result. I sit in the darkness. Subtle noises rustle and groan in its depths.

James?

If he's here, he doesn't answer. The house feels empty. Has he gone back across the street, to Mursey's house?

Tomorrow, I think. He'll come back and wake me up and then we'll leave. Tomorrow this will be over. My life is not what I thought it was, and I am the embryo of a new person. I'm ready for the past to be incinerated; I want my brain taken out and scraped clean, all the false parts cored out.

* * *

After a pack of large, feral housecats crosses the road, I start walking again. I go down past the playground, carrying my rod and tackle; the world is a pleasant, muted green. The neighborhood is full of people, all hidden in their houses. The sun shines, but not blindingly. Leaving the development, I come to the deserted park, with its little green-black pond. Pale, red-tipped plants rise in the shallows of the pond. I walk out on the narrow, eight-foot pier, kneeling to assemble my fishing rod. I bait the hook with a night crawler that squirms, then drop my line in. Friendly mosquitoes land on the surface of the pond, making tiny ripples with their feet.

Only a moment passes—then a great thrashing starts in the water, a glittering disturbance. He is strong and I feel his desperation. The water's only a few feet deep, and I can see the bottom if I look straight down. I can see my fish, a flashing, fighting piece of silver. I pull him thrashing from the water.

I take the fish in my hand. Smaller than I thought, not fully grown. Now comes the distasteful part. I have to watch him die. I set him down on the wooden boards. I try to ignore his suffocating; the trick is to just look away.

He flops his tail, gasps. I begin to feel guilty. He isn't a very big fish. His jaw jerks. His gasping is weak, spasmodic. I know if he dies now I'll feel guilty and I won't enjoy eating him. So I knock him back in the water. A flash of silver; he's gone.

In a year or two, I may catch him again. But for now he can swim, grow. Mosquitoes dance across the surface. Huge birds wheel in the pastel sky. I notice something ten feet from the pier, on the shallow floor of the pond. A strip of silver in the soft mud. I lean down, squint, try to see. But I already know. My fish, already dead, discarded on the bottom of the pond. He made it about ten feet in his death throes.

It is all rather pointless, I suppose. I feel guilty for having waited. I feel guilty for having looked away as he suffocated. I wonder if pond creatures can feel pain or fear. I go home and have lunch.

Morning

SUNLIGHT TEASES ME TOWARD CONSCIOUSNESS. It's streaming in the glass doors.

Uttering some incoherent, strangled noise, I sit bolt upright. James never woke me. But he was here during the night, although the living room is empty now: the arm of the leather armchair is scarred black from cigarettes, and an open aspirin bottle sits on the lamp table. Near the bottle are two—no, three—blue-tinted plastic bags that have been torn apart and licked clean. I hurriedly tug my shoes on.

James? You here?

As my head swims with rising panic—how close *is* the fire? is that smoke and burning plastic I smell?—I get to my feet and go into the hall.

James?

There is no question the neighborhood is now burning; I smell it—I smell burning plastic and think of the playground on fire. I check the kitchen but he is not there. And not in the dining room either. I go upstairs and, going from room to room, get an eerie sense of déjà vu—it is yesterday, and I am wandering the neighborhood, drifting through deserted houses.

I check all bedrooms. Then I go back downstairs and with a sinking feeling admit to myself the obvious: if James is still around, I guess I have a pretty good idea of where to find him.

Before leaving the house, I retreat for a breathless moment into the bathroom. A shiver ripples through me as I splash cold water on my face, and I notice that my injured hand is swollen worse, blue and violet. My eyes are bloodshot, my head's thudding, and I don't know what I'll find outside the front door.

Back in the hallway, I almost pick up my backpack—then decide to leave it behind. If the fire gets this far, let it have everything.

I go to the front door, wryly remembering the fire safety tips they gave us back in the first grade—*always tap the door handle to see if it's hot*. I do. It's warm. I twist it.

The blast of hot air that hits me as I open the door makes me recoil for a moment. But then I step out onto the lawn, in awe of the world. The sky is dark and windy, but there's no rain. The landscape is something from an ominous dream.

Ashes hide the sun and a raccoon shuffles across the grass. Behind the houses across the street, the neighborhood is on fire. With less to feed on, it must have fragmented, zigzagging in opportunistic leaps. Maple trees are burning, and heavy, shifting winds drag tentacles of flame to fresh branches; the wind is feeding them as they leap from trees to bushes, along hedges, engulfing doghouses, wooden fences. The wind, which carries a bitter odor of smoldering vinyl, is stronger, as if a storm is gathering. Houses are on fire, and the trees in Coach Mursey's backyard are burning. A plane bisects the sky, dragging a red trail of fire retardant. Sirens moan. I hear human voices crying out—the red smear of a fire engine cruises down the street a block over. Ash-stained men in overalls jog between houses, carrying shovels.

As I cross the street, a false wind swirls around me—the breath of the fire—blowing ashes up my nose, making me choke. I get to Coach Mursey's lawn, then stop. Terrible curiosity pulls me toward the fire; I must get a good look at it. I step around the side of Mursey's house.

And there it is.

The fire is something mythic. Nightmarish, obscene. The main blaze is throwing spot fires forward to burn treetops and bushes, then advancing to fill the gaps. It has swept over the cornfield and is roaring into the neighborhood. A few houses that I can see are already engulfed by flame, which dances on them in victory, throwing up its arms to the sky, vomiting a great filthy column of smoke. A firefighter half a block away seems to look in my general direction as he jogs toward the fire—but doesn't register my presence at all.

Startled nonetheless, I go backwards and up the porch. The front door is open. I duck under the yellow tape and close the door behind me. My panting, in the close darkness, sounds ferociously loud. The house feels uninhabited.

FIRES

James?

James?

The living and dining rooms are empty, dark and soft with shadows—and although the kitchen is too, I find the basement door open. Catching my breath, I descend. Ruined light is streaming weakly through the basement window, falling on tools, benches, shelves, old furniture upholstered with dust. The little door in the wall is shut. Kneeling, knees in the dust, I undo the three locks and shove it open. On all fours I crawl into the reeking darkness. A flick of my lighter reveals bare walls, naked concrete; I am alone.

I crawl back out, pocket my lighter, and go up to the kitchen. I don't for a second believe that he actually left without me. I go into the hall.

After a moment's hesitation, I climb the stairs. In the upstairs hallway, I pause and listen. Underneath everything I hear the faraway coal-engine voice of the fire. There is a door across from me and I open it. The bathroom. Naked, stripped bare. In my house, this door leads to the bathroom, too. I go down the hall.

James?

Another door. In my house it would be my parents' bedroom. I push it slowly open.

The room is dark, blanketed in dust. Empty except for a stuffed elk's head with black glassy eyes and grotesque hairless patches lying on the bare floor. I close the door.

Further down the hall is a third door, a door that would be mine. On the carpet outside it lie small white things—animal teeth. From behind the door come no sounds. A fear possesses me. That Coach Mursey has come back, that he's behind this door, calmly gathering his belongings, his books and photographs, to save them from the fire. I will open the door and he will devour me, a monster from a children's story. I open the door.

ANTOSCA

With a terrible sensation of calm, I enter. In the swampy darkness, there sits, beast-like, a king-size bed. It has been stripped and its nudity looks obscene. A heavy, medieval iron sword is mounted above the bed; there's a holy cross etched on the blade. Propped against one wall in noble repose, paws planted close together, is a dead Dalmatian. The taxidermy was disturbingly amateurish; the dog's skin looks glued on. On the wall hangs a framed, embroidered sampler which says, in green stitching, *In mysterious ways His wonders He works.*

James sits on the bed.

He's facing away from me, shirtless, the white kabuki mask pushed up onto his forehead. Shoulders slumped. I am filled with gentle, unexpected sympathy, as if for a large animal that has been wounded. But anger, too.

You didn't wake me up, I accuse.

He turns to look at me, red-eyed and regretful.

I know, he sighs. What can I say? There's no excuse.

Yeah, well. We better go, you think?

I don't know how it got this late.

There is a softness to him, like his muscles withered during the night. I come around the other side of the bed, glancing out the window as I do: the world is burning. Only then do I look back at him—and see the gun. He's holding it in his lap, a black handgun, small and docile like a toy.

Is that real? I ask.

No. It's a kid's thing. I found it in one of the houses.

I laugh. Sure it's not real? Did you test it out?

No, I found it in a kid's room.

There is a pause. In this pause I feel a sort of patient assurance settle over me. He is a wreck and I will have to coax him, but we are going to get out of this okay.

You all right to walk? I ask.

FIRES

Walk where?

Um. Away from the fire.

I've been walking all night.

Well, James, you're gonna have to walk more, okay? Time we head out.

I got all shaken up after you went to sleep, he says. I went outside to see the fire, although I had to keep hiding from the firefighters—they're everywhere now, did you see?

The mask slides down partway over his eyes and he pushes it back up. His face is pale, confused. He smells like cigarettes.

Around 4 AM, he says, the coke just sort of melted something away and I suddenly understood what I came here to do.

Yeah?

His hands sort of absently toy with the gun. He does something to it without looking—it makes a hard clicking sound.

My chest tightens up. I thought that gun was a toy, James.

Oh, right. He sighs. Well, the truth comes out. The truth comes out!

Jesus Christ—James, put that thing down and let's fucking get out of here.

He gives me an irritated glance. You know why I came here?

I can guess.

Well, I couldn't do it. I have the gun and I still just couldn't do it. And after a while the sun came up and I looked out the window and there's the fire. I don't know where the time went.

The flames make a sound that puts me in mind of approaching sleep. And we are in here, in a place of soft darkness where it seems necessary to speak in whispers. Again the mask slips down his forehead, but instead of reaching up to push it back, he slides it over his face, hiding himself.

Can you set the gun down? I ask. I don't want either of us getting shot. Now, I hate to *push* you, but we need to get out of here.

He does not set the gun down. Shaking his head, he says, It's so hot.

'It's so hot'? Yeah, uh, that's right. Let's go, James.

I'm not going yet.

Shadows lie all around us like a carpet of leaves. On some level I am calm, but the adrenaline is pumping now, is really burning through my veins. Outside the window, an oak tree in the backyard is on fire.

No, James, you are. Get up. Let's get out of here.

Look, man, he says. You just go on ahead, I'll come later.

Let's go, you're coming now.

Later, he says.

The kabuki mask conceals whatever reaction there might be. He could be a mannequin. Actually, he's sitting uncannily still, but I have the unsettling, illogical impression that he's in motion, that he's moving somewhere at dangerous speeds.

Is Ruth waiting for you? he asks.

What?

I wonder, he says, when I walk out, who's waiting for me?

James. *Let's fucking go.*

He jabs the gun at me, alarmingly. *Fuck* you, he says. Get down there, get out of this house. There's no reason for you to be here.

Seeing that he has gotten a reaction—I flinched, I backed off—he lowers the gun.

You don't deserve her, he says. She could have helped me, you know. She really could have. But she's selfish. A manipulator.

Fine, I say. Sure.

It was real serious between me and her. Real serious.

Fine. It doesn't matter. Let's go.

And she didn't just leave me. Not just once. She'd been leaving me for a while but she kept coming back. She couldn't get *quite enough*. Nobody knew how to hurt her like I did.

You know what? I say, stepping forward aggressively, chills suddenly rising up below my skin (maybe that's adrenaline, plain rage, whatever, but just for a second it makes me not afraid of the gun). Why don't you *shut the fuck up.*

He sighs. The fact that he doesn't acknowledge the perceptible rise in my nerve deflates that same rise and for a moment I just stand there, unsure.

She knew how much power she had, he says.

A fetid silence descends. My sympathy has gone away and I feel nothing but ugliness toward him. For just a second I think of fresh red bruises on Ruth's neck, her breasts.

James, come *on*, get up.

When she met you, he says, I don't even know what I wanted to do. I couldn't believe you were replacing me. *Again.*

You have certain strange, stupid ideas in your head, I tell him. *Again?* Stop…deluding yourself. These are fantasies produced by your broken mind, you understand?

Oh, *no*, he suddenly yells at me. No, they're *not*. They're *realities* suppressed by your terrified *memory*. And she saw through that! Because you know what she needs to get off. Do you hurt her? Hurt her for me.

Furious, I reach forward and rip the mask off his face, which is drawn tight with rage, blood flowering under the skin at his cheekbones, lips pulled back in pure, childlike hatred. His hands, one of which holds the gun, are trembling in his lap. I try to control myself.

James, I say. Don't say another word.

But his face is blotched with rage. Get the fuck out of here, right now, he orders. Go back. Go back to faking it.

Fuck it, I am leaving. *Without* you. And if you live through today—

ANTOSCA

My hand lashes forward and grips his throat, compressing his windpipe.

—don't you *ever*—

He jerks away—then twists and hits me in the side of the head so hard reality stutters. I reel sideways. I taste vomit. When the curtains of darkness are yanked up, I see James still sitting on the bed, watching me, and it seems I'm on the floor. When he realizes I'm definitely conscious, he slides the mask back on his face and kneels over me, gun dangling from one fist, and says,

That felt incredibly cathartic for me.

I punch him in the throat and grab for the gun.

There is a jagged, inelegant fight. I claw at the eye holes of the mask. The gun slams my ear, again and again, like a stone. The side of my head feels wet. His other hand is gripping my hair, impossibly strong. My struggling turns defensive. I glimpse clenched teeth. I try to pull free but end up doubled on the floor, gagging, coughing blood from a blow to the neck. In the background, his panting seems amplified. I look up.

There's a sudden concussion, like a bomb going off near my left eye, which bleaches everything, which deadens my forehead, which all at once makes my skull weigh a thousand tons.

The ceiling is a colorless space. Neon bacteria swim in my eyes. A nasal tone, like a tuning fork, teases me and I smell burnt, bitter gunpowder. My forehead is granite. The ceiling is cream colored.

My eyes flick around the room. Smeared, disparate images. He's standing over me, kabuki-masked. The drone of the tuning fork covers all other sounds.

James looks down at me. I blink. Am I dying? Can he see that I'm not dead? I wonder if he'll help me up. I try to reach out to him. My arms are heavy, sluggish.

FIRES

Oh, he mumbles, the words barely audible. Oh, wow.

He edges toward the door. The last I see of him is a dark blur at the top of my vision.

Feet go down the stairs. The front door closes.

Agonizingly, I raise my skull. I crawl to the foot of the bed. The bedpost is slippery but I get my fingers around it. It takes two or three minutes to get to my feet. I don't feel connected to my limbs. My neck aches like it's packed with coals. I smell all kinds of smoke.

I stagger to the door and rest there, listing to one side, my breathing ragged. My head feels like a giant blood blister. I reel into the hallway and manage to grab the banister instead of falling down the stairs. I take them one at a time.

Trouble locating the front door. It's only about fifteen feet from the stairs, but somehow I find myself in the kitchen, and from there I go back into the hall and am unexpectedly looking at my reflection in the mirror. I'm calm, something's spreading over me, heavy dullness.

In the mirror, I see the dime-sized black hole over my left eye. Blood is just beginning to ooze out. A red abrasion ring circles the wound. Broken veins in my eyeball stain the eye red. I try to wipe ashes from my face, but the ashes won't go away, because they are powder burns.

The powder burns don't hurt.

The front lawn's pitching and rolling. There is moaning; it is coming from me. A hot wind burns my lungs, but as it's like being on Novocain and having wisdom teeth pulled: you just don't care. A tree in the neighbors' yard burns with simple majesty. Trees in my own yard, across the street, are burning too. Everything is crackling, popping. Wind tugs the blaze.

I should be terrified.

I'm not.

I take hesitant steps. My left eye is blurry and the right one is watering from smoke. But I don't feel angry, upset, or frightened. The pleasant deadness in my skull grows stronger. Firefighters' voices are behind me.

I see something moving on the lawn a few feet ahead. Something small, the size of a wrist. It squirms in the grass, curling up on itself like a huge, damaged red ant. The thing has red flesh and a rat-like, stringy tail. A squirrel. Whose hair has been scorched off, whose skin is blistered and sloughing. Black eyes roll back in its skull. It tries to dig a hole.

My feet drag as I stumble across the road. Weird, drugged happiness makes me grin and laugh. Ash-smeared firefighters run down nearby streets.

I cross my lawn. Burning trees toss firebrands at me. Branches land near my feet, on fire. Pretty soon *my* house is going to be on fire. Fine by me.

The sky is a storm of carbon and wobbling heat. Ash eddies in the air. I breathe fumes—a vapor of melting deck chairs, Coke bottles, bicycles, Barbie dolls. I touch the crispy, dime-sized hole in my head.

I walk into a backyard.

Spot fires are already coming to life here. The wind gives them oxygen. Near the garden is a child's toy box, brown and dirt-caked, like a little coffin. Curious, I kick it open.

Inside lie dolls. Some are naked and some are in gowns. Some are whole and some lack limbs. There are other toys, too—dinosaurs and wolves, things like that.

FIRES

After I cross another street, I sit by some boxwood bushes, where maybe the firefighters won't notice me.

It's difficult to keep my head upright. Blood drips on my hand. Coming from my forehead, but surprisingly insubstantial. I wipe it off and dig in my pocket for a crushed, almost empty pack of cigarettes. Inserting one in my mouth, I find myself unable to locate my lighter. A spot fire has grown in the bushes just across the street. It is looking for a way to leap across.

I get to my feet, walk over to the fire, and lean down to let it lick the tip of my cigarette. Sighing smoke, I return to my spot by the boxwoods and sit down again.

With a fine view of the burning, I enjoy a leisurely smoke. It seems almost eternal, this moment. I am flooded with emphatic feelings of wellbeing and newness.

When finally the fire gets too close, I heave myself to my feet again and stumble in the opposite direction, nonchalant. I see a swimming pool, big and deep, surrounded by deck chairs.

A skin of ash floats on the water, clinging to my jeans as I wade in. In three or four feet of water, I stop. It might be a bad idea, I decide, to let water get in the bullet hole. A warm, freewheeling wind tugs the water's surface.

How strange that I should have ever been scared of the fire. Now it has come and everything is being destroyed, and that doesn't bother me at all. Ashes swirl over my head. Lives, histories.

Black smoke rises from the nearest house.

The bushes around me are on fire, too. Spot fires leap forward, great batches of flame picked up and tossed by the wind. When the long vivid tongues flap and dance in the breeze, it's like they're waving at me. My lungs blister.

Beautiful blue-black smoke gluts the sky.

A gigantic figure of ash emerges from the scenery. A huge man, a terrifying shape. It lurches toward the swimming pool, shoving a deck chair out of its way, wiping a black-smeared face. From across the water it stares at me, disbelieving.

Get out of the water! The hell you doing in there?

I have difficulty forming words. Incredulously, the smoke jumper walks toward me.

You all right? he inquires. Can you get out on your own?

I stare at him. I've been shot, I try to say, dragging syllables all over the place.

Come on, he barks. Get outta there. You'll be burned alive.

I try to haul myself out of the water, but fail, so the smoke jumper gets his blackened bear-paws under my armpits and begins to pull me up, grunting with exertion.

You aren't supposed to *be* here anymore, he says.

Floating

WHAT HAPPENS NOW IS NOT SO IMPORTANT. It's blurry. I'm not cogent, not observant, as I'm carried down burning streets. As I lie in a field waiting for the helicopter. As I'm flown through swirling smoke, under gathering clouds, to the hospital. As an IV is spiked into my vein. As I lie quietly under white cotton sheets until I am wheeled into surgery.

Hospital

FROM INSIDE MY THUDDING DARKNESS, I see the eastern sky changing. I see it in the window, from my crisp white bed. My head sledge-

FIRES

hammers. There's a coat of blood on the horizon.

It begins suddenly, without preamble. Hard pellets of rain banging against the windows. A low, windy, moan. A gathering roar.

I wake in the night as my blood pressure is being taken. My IV is empty and the nurse changes it. The pounding of the rain is hypnotic at first but soon becomes painful, unbearable.

The rain continues through morning. For a little while, there's a hint of sun. Then just rain. A heathery gray sky, and rain.

When the two doctors come, they have to speak over the rattling of the windows. It never ends, the rattling, like someone's trying to get in. They tell me I'll need physical therapy. A plate in my skull. The bullet's still there; safer to leave it in.

My parents come later with strands of wet hair stuck to their foreheads. I'm out of intensive care, in a normal hospital room. There's a second bed next to mine, empty. My parents are distraught, bewildered. What am I doing here? they want to know. I tell them to go home, forgetting that home is a husk. At night they go back to their motel.

The rain goes on.

I'm alone. Intensely, perfectly alone. I like it, though, being alone. It doesn't bother me anymore. My nose begins to bleed.

The place feels like a womb, and I float, curled humbly on my side, in the aquatic darkness. Sometimes the nurses give morphine. The morphine makes it difficult to piss. From time to time, I touch my head, most of which has been shaved down to stubble by the surgeons.

It is so pleasant to be alone. Who was that person who feared this?

Two detectives with interchangeable damp faces come to interview me. One of my doctors leans against the wall while I am being questioned. They want to know about James. They want to know about the gunshot. They want to know about what happened.

Why did he shoot you?

Did he shoot me? I don't remember much, an accident maybe. We were messing around with the gun.

Why'd you have the gun?

I don't know. It was his.

Where were you? When he shot you?

I don't know. Outside?

I have no desire to cooperate with these detectives. I want nothing to do with prosecuting James. I have no anger toward him, no need for revenge. It is inevitable, I think, that he will go free and continue to stalk his nightmares.

I will exonerate James with silence. I will not mention Ruth, or George Mursey. I will not tell them about James and Mursey—that would be an extraordinary betrayal.

How could fire exist in this world? Outside the window, there's just a boneless gray dusk stretching to the soft muted shapes of the Appalachians, which are made of the same stuff as the sky.

When I am alone, my mind looks toward a strange liminal place, toward a kind of blissful reminiscence of what I've seen.

But I'm afraid to go. My mind seems fragile. Soon, but not yet.

I can't eat much, can't keep anything down. My nourishment comes from the long, umbilical, intravenous line that snakes across the bed and disappears into my left forearm.

The noise of the phone ringing is like glass being ground and crushed beside my eardrums. I reach across the bed for it.

Yeah? Hello?

Hey. Jon?

Who's this?

It's James.

My whole body flinches; I jolt upright. But then I realize I simply don't give a shit. That person who got shot is dead and gone. And James's voice seems to be coming to me from across an unbridgeable distance. This must be what a fetus hears of the outside world.

I don't really have anything to say to you, James.

Listen—I'm at a pay phone. By the grocery. I haven't been arrested or anything, but they held me for a day and they keep questioning me. They told me not to leave Bondurant. But I'm about to.

There is a dead pause before he speaks again.

Listen. I think the gun was, uh. Really old or something, because it just, you know. There was probably something wrong with the, ah. Firing pin. You know?

Silence, and then, again—Jon? You know?

I tell him: Sure, man.

You really don't remember anything. Do you.

Oh, I remember you shooting me in the head. Yeah, I remember that.

When I was watching Mursey's house, senior year, I saw you come out of there one night.

No you didn't.

You walked out of his front door, crossed the street, and went into your house.

No.

We have a bond, he says. There's a kind of bond.

I don't know that there is, James.

Sure there is, he says. We're friends.

I am silent, and abruptly he hangs up. I feel anger. No I don't. I don't feel anger. I don't feel fear. Let him make things up if he needs to. I push those things down because I am very good at pushing things down. And I set the receiver on its cradle and nestle into bed again, curling into a peaceful, fetal position. Did that happen? Did I just dream that conversation?

By now, the land must be uniformly sponge-like. It has rained relentlessly for days, and I imagine toadstools growing out of nearby streets, moss growing on cars, everything rusting in the city, dirty lakes forming in the burned-out wreckage of my old neighborhood.

Stoically, as though thinking of some myth that I never finished reading, I wonder where Coach Mursey is now. I envision him as a human shape made of ash, traveling across a country made of ashes. With his every step, a piece of the world rises and blows away. Trees, dogs, other people—all shapes swarming in the ash. The landscape is torn apart and remade each day by a choking wind. Everything is ruin, yet everything continues. Mursey begins a new life, with a new dog, a great grey wolfhound.

But, unexpectedly, this fantasy is comforting. Because if human beings were made of ash, they could be remade at a touch. But this is not how things are. To be made new takes time. I know that now.

The sun rises as I am drowsing in the recliner; the gold-redness of morning cups my face. During the night, the rain ended. I am waiting, exquisitely alone, for breakfast.

The door whispers open.

Jon?

Languidly, my pain a distant tug, I turn. Ruth, soft-eyed and hesitant, lingers by the door.

Jon?

Her face is tired—has she traveled all night?—and her hair is in tangles. Neither of us speaks as I look back at her, struck by her beauty in the way one admires a girl in a photograph; there is a dark, palpable distance. The fear and concern in her eyes are like faraway searchlights, seen through fog.

Hey, babe, I say.

She murmurs, They shaved your head. Oh, god.

Yeah. And stitches.

Oh, Jon. I mean, how are you? What a question . . .

I'm fine. Drugged.

She sighs. She sighs, also sensing the disconnectedness between us—or, rather, *my* disconnection from her—and I see a blush of humiliated desperation rise in her face. Something resembling pity fills me, as though I'm sitting at a window, unseen, and watching a mother look for her lost baby.

I need some of those drugs, she says. I've been so scared. I didn't sleep at all on the way down.

Get a needle, I slur. We'll take some blood out of me. And put it in you.

I'd like that, she says quietly. I would like to have your blood in me.

Nervous, she comes around the bed, closer to me. I am confused about whether I want this. Now she leans down and, afraid of touching my shaved and bandaged head, kisses my hand, my wrist. She strokes the place where the IV goes in. I watch her heart-shaped face, her slender arms. The pain in her face shames me, and I can't look away from it.

Look at you, she says, opening her palm toward my forehead as if to draw the bullet out by sorcery. Look at you. Look at you.

I don't look so pretty anymore, do I?

She makes an effort to laugh. She closes her eyes tightly, then opens them again, pressing her fingers together and turning them against her pursed lips.

No, she says, you look like a puppy who somebody kicked half to death.

That must be appealing.

ANTOSCA

It's heartbreaking, actually. You look so—helpless. It makes me want to hold you and take care of you. Until you're happy and healthy.

Suddenly I have a strange and familiar sensation; it is a very specific feeling, one of discovery and renewal, of fortune leaning in to bestow a kiss. It is familiar because it comes so rarely, and such memories are vivid. It's how I felt when I met her.

I want to know you, she says. And I want you to know me. My life. I want to tell you all of it.

I am silent. Through the insulation of my silence, I feel her reaching out to me, fumbling for me. I see her not from a distance, but with an intimacy that takes nothing for granted. There are moments when you look at someone and understand you could fall into that person like light into a prism and be changed.

But she is a reminder of the person I used to be, and so I'm wary. And, for a moment, I keep silent.

What are you thinking? she says softly, with a note of forlorn fear.

Nothing.

Do you—not want me here? she asks.

Oh, no, I say finally. I want you here. I need you. More than morphine, even.

She laughs and sighs. Sun is in her face. A silence, intimate and sad, descends on us. Old rainwater drips on the window ledge, gently tapping. I think distantly that what seems like silence is never entirely silent. And I'm suddenly aware of how necessary she is.

Again she leans forward to touch my wrist, pressing her fingers into the flesh experimentally, as if it is clay which she will soon be molding.

Look at you, she murmurs.

Doubts come to me, but I ignore them. I don't want to be conflicted now. There is sun on my skin and some good liquor in my veins.

The heart is full of silence, I think, but rarely silent. I have never felt this willing to love someone. I want to love her without doubts or secrets. So I force them down.

Jon, she murmurs, I love you, but I don't understand. I don't understand what happened here. Can you explain this to me? Please?

The melted sun warms us. It captures single, delicate filaments of her hair. It clings to everything, sticky and drowsy. It warms the naked bed across the room, which is being prepared for a new patient.

. . . And the air is redolent with a kind of hazy, luminous misery as the sun crawls higher; and the warm, buttery sunlight grows diluted. Frail shadows return. And we linger in shade the color of white wine, and in her dark brown eyes there are still questions I don't want to face. And so I turn my head, slightly, and go somewhere else.

Burning Leaves

I AM BACK IN MY NEIGHBORHOOD; I watch it burn. The flames are playful, and I am not afraid. Crouched by the boxwood bushes, I smoke a cigarette as I watch the history of my life take to the wind as ashes. I smell vinyl siding and melted Barbie dolls in the smoke-dark air. Ashes float down, coating my arms.

I don't know why—perhaps the trauma of the bullet has caused my brain to hemorrhage endorphins—but I am cheerful. No, not just cheerful. Nearly euphoric. Black smoke, spilling ashes from its guts, billows from my house, and this is one of the happiest moments of my life. I can smell histories burning, and in this landscape of homes the person I was lies like a snakeskin, waiting to be incinerated.

Shifting winds throw great dark handfuls of ash over the neighborhood, and I am watching a red-black monster ransack the museum of an American childhood. But it's not upsetting or frightening. I watch it all go up in gorgeous flame.

And I smell all the old playgrounds burning.

AUTHOR'S NOTE

I am grateful for the advice, friendship, and encouragement of the following people: Jennifer Banash and Willy Blackmore at Impetus, John Crowley, Elaine Han, Ted Dawes, Caitlin Taylor, Helen Oyeyemi, Ned Vizzini, Alex Remington, Marty Beckerman, Diala Shamas, and Steve, Mary, and Gianmarco Antosca.

ABOUT THE AUTHOR

Nick Antosca lives, works, and writes on the East Coast of the United States of America. He was born in the state of Louisiana